CHOSEN WOLF

IRON BEAST PACK

ANGELICA AQUILES

Chosen Wolf

Copy/Line Editing: Heather Fox at Fox Proof Editing

Cover Design: Francesca Michelon at MerryBookRound

Formatting by: November Sweets

Thank you to all my lovely readers for giving the Iron Beast Pack Series a chance. It means the world to me that you went on this journey with me. I hope I make you all proud with the ending.

TRIGGER WARNING

Please be aware that this is a Why Choose Romance so the main character will have more than one love interest. Possible triggers may include blood play, and light BDSM. This book contains adult content and mature language. It is intended for readers 18+.

Enjoy!

CHOSEN WOLF

Chapter 1

Kat

"A wolf?" I shout, not believing my own words. How is this possible? There is just no way.

My voice echoes through the small room in the cabin. Everyone flinches, and I watch as Zay stifles the need to cover his ears and brings his hands down stiffly to his sides.

"How the hell is she a *wolf*?" I grind my teeth in disbelief, but deep down, I'm fearful for what my daughter will have to go through. My own transformation was the most painful thing I have ever endured, even more so than giving birth to my children.

My wolf paces around her area nervously. It's quiet, the pounding of my heart and Ava's cries are the only things I hear. I inspect her neck for bite marks, not quite touching her. I don't want to cause her any more pain, but there's no sign of trauma. Her skin looks untouched.

The smell of fresh linen and the tranquility of this cabin is the opposite of my current situation. I'm drenched in blood, and so are my guys. I want nothing more than to scrub away the death and destruction of the last few hours, but the image of my blood-coated dagger comes to mind every time I close my eyes. In the moments between my daughter's pained wails, I can still hear the sound of metal striking bone as the guys and I plunged The Kiss of Death through Krissy mere moments ago.

My mind hasn't had time to process what happened to the two people I watched die tonight, and even in this new world of magic and shifters, I wasn't ready to experience a sea of spirits fighting alongside us. I'm not sure anyone could ever be ready for an army of ghosts.

To my right, Az holds Cash back, the youngest of the guys, and he looks like he's going to murder anyone that gets near Ava. To my left, Tyler is holding onto Zay while his body practically vibrates to reach my daughter.

Benji is on one side of the bed, and Bryson and Ryder are on the opposite side, talking to each other in a hushed tone. Their faces are red and strained, and they look as if they're ready to kill. I want to ask what they're talking about, but a scream brings my attention back to my daughter.

She looks pale with dark circles surrounding her eyes. Her lips are cracked and have begun to bleed.

Tears stream down her face, and her eyes aren't focusing on anything. Her body looks weak and ready to give out. I know that feeling.

I'm lost, and I don't know what to do to help Ava. I know she's strong, but I don't want this for her.

She was acting strange the last couple of days, and she

hid in her room and didn't want to come out. Is this why she was avoiding me?

I turn around and look at Ash since he's the one who told me about humans turning into wolves.

"How is this possible without a bite?" I demand, but he looks just as startled as I am—as we all are. If he doesn't know, who else can I ask? I look around the room again, but no one seems to know what's going on.

"Are there any theories, wolf?" She's watching everything with vigilant eyes, but she's just as confused as the rest of us.

I walk to the end of the bed and touch her leg but immediately pull back. She's burning up. I look at my blistered palm in shock. How is she still alive if she's this hot? Did this happen to me too?

Ryder takes a chair and throws it out the window in frustration, and the crash of glass shattering leaves a stunned silence around the room. His fists are opening and closing. Everyone seems shocked by Ryder's unexpected breakdown. He's usually calm and relaxed. Ash moves to restrain him before he can launch something else out of the broken window, but someone speaks up.

"Alphas." I look up at Bryson. He's got a pained look on his face. "Can we comfort her?"

The guys look at me, waiting for my answer, but I have no clue what Bryson means. "Someone explain it to me," I groan. It really has been a long day, and watching Ava in so much pain is the icing on the cake. I'm barely holding on to the scream of frustration burning in my chest.

Everyone looks at Ash, and he closes his eyes and rubs them. "They want to comfort Ava."

"Umm . . ." Ryder, Bryson, Zay, and Cash are all bouncing in anticipation of my answer. "What exactly does that mean?" I fold and unfold my hands, not sure what else to do.

"We lay in bed together. Us being close will help her transition." I almost say fuck no, but then remember how painful and lonely it felt for me. If this helps my daughter, how could I turn it down? "Why would you guys be able to help?" But then I lift my hand so they don't answer. "You know what? Never mind," I say. I have a sinking feeling low in my stomach, and I think I know what this is about. "No funny business from any of you guys," I say, and everyone lets out a relieved breath like they were expecting me to say no.

"We'll behave," Ryder says with sincerity.

"Really?" Ash scrunches his brow. I smile sadly at him because it feels like every day my kids need me less and less.

"Yeah. Let's get you cleaned up," Benji says gently. "There's nothing more you can do here." Leaving my daughter in this state, with a group of boys who are practically strangers, is the last thing I want to do.

When I make no motion to move, someone else speaks up.

"Kat, staring at your daughter will only make it worse for you and her." I close my eyes, taking a moment for myself before opening them back up. Benji stands behind me, rubbing my shoulders. I'd rather bring Krissy back to life and fight her a hundred times over than watch my daughter writhe in pain and not be able to help her.

Benji gently nudges me forward, and as my wolf's aggression eases with his touch, I let him guide me toward the door.

"If you guys need us, we'll be at the house," I say more to myself than to the room of anxious boys surrounding my daughter.

Az and Tyler let go of Cash and Zay, and they waste no time moving away from them.

"I'll stay here with them," Ash says, but I can only manage a grim smile of thanks. "I'll call you if she needs you."

It kills me to leave her alone.

Ash looks like he wants to talk to me about something, but I shake my head. Not right now. I'm not ready. There's too much going on to even think about anything but Ava.

I walk out of the cabin, wondering how the hell my daughter turned into a shifter and how this will impact her life.

The air in the cabin feels stagnant as soon as the front door slams shut behind Kat, or maybe it's just the distance between me and my mate that feels so suffocating. *Mate.* I don't think I'll ever get tired of calling her that. After the day she came to my room, I knew we had to be something more. I can't get enough of her. I want my scent all over her clothes, her room, her bed sheets so everyone knows she belongs to me. I don't know how I'm going to keep my hands to myself after we mate.

Visions of her naked body tied to my bed and inside my car send my heart racing. I want to watch her bleed as I tease her body and she comes all over my dick, my hands, my mouth. I want to watch as my brothers fuck her and mark her. She belongs to us. The outcasts. The Iron Beast Pack.

Soon, I tell myself over and over again, trying to focus on the scene in front of me. Even if I had gone home with

Kat, now isn't the time to get her naked and mark every inch of her body.

She's had a rough day—we all have. After so many years of wanting to catch Krissy and break the curse, she's finally dead. We should be celebrating what we've accomplished, but for some reason, happiness doesn't feel like our reality right now. Not with Kat's daughter twisting in agony in front of me, and not with Krissy's last words still bouncing around my brain.

Before she died, she told us that she was hired by the council to kill Kat and take the powers of all their ancestors. She said she was promised all the power and that they would rule together. I thought she meant that she would rule alongside her sister at first, but the way she spoke to a voice inside her head made it obvious that she wasn't the brains of this operation. Someone was pulling her strings the entire time, but who, and why did they use her specifically? What was the real purpose for taking her ancestors' magic, and now that she's gone, who will be coming for us next?

"Ahhh—" another high-pitched scream pulls me from my thoughts, and I immediately swing into action. I walk into the linen closet and grab a small towel, then move to the bathroom and turn the sink faucet on freezing cold.

I bring the cold, wet towel back to Ava, and all the men stare at me and growl. I know how they're feeling. It's the same way when someone gets too close to Kat. They want to protect her, but they're still so young and truly don't know how to help her.

They've never seen someone transition. It baffles me how Kat did it all by herself.

I place the wet towel on her forehead to cool her down a bit. Her body responds to the shift in temperature and relaxes, but only slightly.

"Would you have cared for her mother?" my wolf asks. That stops me for a moment because in all honesty, I don't think I would have. Maybe I would have felt a little bad for her suffering, but I thought she was more of a nuisance than anything, and that realization upsets me.

"From this day forward," I tell my wolf. *"We'll make it up to Kat anyway we can."* That's the truth. I may not be able to change the past, but I can change the future.

"Fuck off, Ryder," Zay says, knocking into his friend's shoulder. "I'm lying down next to her." They push and shove like children, but I let them handle their own shit. I'm not here to interfere with what they have going on. I'm only here to help Ava.

Cash and Zay lie on either side of her, and Cash brings his hand to her stomach. I'm surprised he's keeping it there. Her body is hot to the touch. He's going to need a healer for those blisters, but it looks like he doesn't mind so long as he's close to her.

Her face is against Zay's neck, and he flinches at the touch of her hand on his skin, but other than that, he doesn't move.

She's calming down, so I go into another room and pull out some clean sweats and a shirt. I take off my blood-soaked clothes and throw them in the trash. I don't need a reminder of what happened today or what could have happened if Kat hadn't been able to call her dagger the way she did.

I go back into the bathroom and turn the shower on. I wait for it to get hot and get in, washing off the blood, dirt, and sweat from the day.

Everything is quiet at the moment, so I allow myself five minutes extra to relax my muscles.

When Ava screams again, I get out and dress quickly. As I enter the bedroom and take in the sight before me, my feet falter.

Wait.

I put my palm on the wall to keep me from stumbling.

Something is wrong—very wrong.

She doesn't have her mother's violet eyes, which surprises me because I thought she would have the same power as Kat. Her eyes are as amber as mine and my brothers, but there are hints of black surrounding her irises, and when her eyes widen and turn to me, the amber turns red.

The talons ripping open her skin are not like ours; they're sharp and darker than they should be.

I try to get closer to her, but the guys growl in warning. If I wasn't so shocked, I'd push my way toward her.

The guys don't notice the subtle differences in her appearance. They're so engrossed in helping her survive this that they have no clue that something is wrong.

Her smell . . . is off. It's like the scent of a shifter, but at the same time, it's not.

Something is not right here. I need to talk to the guys

before bringing it up to Kat. I don't want her to panic. Maybe we can figure it out without having to worry our mate even more.

Chapter 3

Kat

I don't think I'll ever be the same person I was before I got here. The old Kat would've never survived the shit I've been through, but this new version of myself that I've had to become is unrecognizable. I'm not sure if this new me is good or bad yet.

I look at the palm of my hand, and it's no longer blistering; my shifter abilities have healed me. Benji stops the car, and without thinking, I open the door to get out.

At the house, pack members are already cleaning the mess. My body sags when I see the scene again, knowing the dead bodies of Krissy and Dan are among all the gore. I don't feel sorry for them, but when I think about the ghosts of Amara's coven, I shiver. I truly hope I don't have to see them ever again.

I smell like copper and death. I'm so sticky and wet, and I'm walking like I'm wearing a thousand pounds of bricks on my legs. Each step is heavier than the one before.

I move past people as they avoid making eye contact

with me. I don't care to ask why nor do I have the energy to.

"I need to check on Ezra." My voice is low and hollow as I stagger up the porch stairs. I look behind me at the trail of blood I brought with me, and still my body is numb.

Tyler hands me a phone, and I see Ezra's number on the screen. He must have known I was going to ask about my son. It doesn't scare me like it would have that they know my every thought before I can even form the words.

Tyler opens the door to the house, and as I walk in, I stand there for a moment to see if I'm going to break down and cry, but there's nothing. No emotion whatsoever. Does this mean I've finally lost my mind?

The living room is bright, clean, and dust free—completely untouched by the mess marring the front lawn. I sigh and turn around to head back outside, not wanting to get specks of my enemies' blood on the couches.

Taking a seat on the porch, I watch the men and women scurry around getting this place to its original state. I almost want to ask if they need help, but my body is too tired to move.

No one glares at me for not doing anything. They don't look like they expect me to help, and that makes me feel slightly better knowing that I don't have to drag my heavy body and clean up the gore.

I press the green button next to Ezra's name and put it on a video call. Before my son answers, I turn to see Tyler and Benji in the doorway and ask, "Where's he staying?"

"With Logan," Tyler says as he and Benji walk out onto the porch and fall down next to me on either side.

"Is Ava going to be okay?" Ezra asks as soon as he answers the video call. Not even a hello, which makes me think he knew what was happening with Ava long before I did.

There's a crease in his brow. He's worried about her. They might fight and complain about each other, but at the end of the day, they're family, and family has each other's backs.

"I'm not sure yet," I say. Benji rubs my leg in comfort, letting me know I'm not alone in this. "Why didn't you tell me there was something wrong with Ava?" I'm too exhausted to sound angry. At this point, I'm starting to think that I might be broken.

Since learning about the supernatural world, it's been nothing but a race to stay on top of everyone who wants to kill me. Is this how it will always be for us? Is this what my daughter has to look forward to? Will she have my magic? Will Ezra have to endure this too?

There are too many questions floating around in my head with barely any answers.

Ezra ends the crackling silence between us with a long exhale. "She told me to keep it a secret, Mom." When I don't answer he says, "It's our code. We don't snitch on each other."

I should have realized sooner that their bond is so much stronger than I ever knew. I guess growing up without siblings doesn't make me very experienced in these things.

"Ezra!" I yell, but my tone is missing its usual bite. "I

need to know these things. How can I protect you if I don't know what's going on?"

"But was there really anything we could've done to prevent this?" my wolf asks, peeking her head out.

"She'll be fine, right?" He tries to sound confident, but there's slight fear in his tone.

I close my eyes for a moment then open them again. "I hope so." I rub my eyes before saying, "Is there anything you want to tell me about yourself?"

"N-No," he stutters. "I'm completely norm . . . uh fine," he corrects himself.

"Ezra, your sister and I are completely normal except for having supernatural abilities. Nothing has changed." But really everything has. It won't be the same, but there is no need to worry him; he's had enough of a scare to last a lifetime.

We say our goodbyes, but when I get up, I fall back down. My body is too tired to move. If I could sleep here, I would, but I need a shower. It's only been a day, but it feels like I've been this dirty for days. The guys wait for me to ask for help, but I won't. I need to feel like I'm still in control, like my life isn't a frazzled mess, and that's why I need to pick myself up.

This time, I manage to pull my body weight all the way up, but when I stumble back a step, there's a steady hand preventing me from falling again. I allow the kind gesture because I know when to be stubborn and when to accept help.

Before I cross to the other side of the door, someone

jogs up behind me. Suddenly there's more adrenaline, and my fight-or-flight instinct returns.

"I got your phone, Luna," The name *Luna* startles me for a second. I want to ask about the odd name but think better of it. Future Kat can worry about that later. My body eases again. Joseph, one of the betas, walks over and hands me the phone.

"Thanks," I tell him gratefully. I grab it and awkwardly try to slide it into my pocket, but then I remember how dirty I am and hold it out away from my body.

In the bathroom, I let the door close gently behind me and nearly scream when I finally face the mirror. I look like the joker from Batman. I'm surprised no one ran away from me. I wonder if that's why the other shifters kept their heads down. I would too if I saw some crazy lady looking the way I do.

I peel off my clothes slowly, inspecting the remnants of healing bruises all over my body in various stages of purple and yellow. Leaning closer to the mirror, I tilt my chin up and gently run my hands across my throat. Ash's finger-prints are faint but still there, a sordid reminder of how he nearly choked me to death.

I walk away from the mirror and start the shower, making sure it's scorching hot. Maybe it'll help me wash off the events of today.

After I shower, I find Ash in my bed. He's cleaned up and wearing nothing but boxers. Beads of water still drip from the tendrils of his platinum hair, and my heart races when I think of those boys alone with Ava while she's so vulnerable.

Before I can even ask what he's doing here, he leans toward me on one elbow and says, "Don't worry, Benji and Tyler are with her now. She's stable."

Sighing in relief, I move toward the bed, but when I get a closer look at the emotion filling his soft blue eyes, he turns his head from me to hide his expression. He has so much to get off his chest, but I'm not in the right state of mind to listen. I've had all I can handle for now. Tomorrow is a different day, and right now, all I want to do is sleep.

I shake my head before saying, "Not tonight, Ash."

He clears his throat and nods. "I had Benji and Tyler send the boys home tonight. They fought them over it, but in the end, they used their alpha voices and the kids couldn't oppose them. Ava needs her rest."

My body sags in relief. I don't know what's going on. I feel like my life is spiraling out of control, and there's no way for me to stop it. It's even worse because I'm bringing my kids along for the ride.

This is not how I envisioned my life going.

"Do you hate it?" my wolf asks sadly.

"No, of course I don't." That's the truth. I'm happier now than I've ever been, but everything seems to be coming all at once. Before I have time to process one thing, another thing shows up, and it's always harder than the last. *"I just . . . I just wished everything worked out different-ly."* I admit.

"I want to go see her." I dry my long purple strands with my towel, once I'm done, I hang it behind the bathroom door.

I go to my drawer to pick out a pair of sweats and a

shirt before bringing them up to my nose and sniffing. They smell like Ash, and I smile at the thought of him stuffing his clothes in my drawers. I don't have to steal—I mean borrow—their belongings anymore.

"How about we call her instead?" Ash asks, I turn back toward him. My face must give away the irritation.

"Her pain has passed and she needs time to process everything. Let her be. She's tired, you're tired. We know she's alive and taken care of. We need the rest. I don't know why, but I have a gut feeling that things will be getting a lot worse."

I agree, but only because my eyelids are so heavy. I think I'm past the point of exhaustion.

Ash looks at his phone and dials a number, setting it on speaker so that I can hear. "Hey, Tyler. Kat wants to talk to Ava."

"Sure thing." I hear some shuffling.

I finish getting dressed quickly and meet Ash in my bed. He places the call on video chat and hands me the phone so that I can see her.

"Hey, Mom," she says, looking as exhausted as I feel. Her voice is raspy and weak. I'm relieved to know that the shifting phase is over. I wonder what her fur color is? But that's a question for another time. I want to make sure she's okay.

"Hey, mija. How are you feeling?" I grip the phone tighter. Fuck what Ash said, I should go visit her.

"Better." She yawns, which makes me do the same.

"Do you want me to come . . ."

"N-no," she stutters, just stay there. "You can see me

tomorrow. I really just want my rest, and I know you need yours too. Doctor Jones is here. He said he'll call you if anything happens to me, but nothing will happen. I'm feeling better already." She tries to sound enthusiastic, but it falls flat.

"Okay." I do trust the doctors here. They kept Benji and Tyler alive while I found a cure to help them.

"I have to tell you something, just not tonight. We all need the rest." I want to push for more, but Ash doesn't let me.

"Come on," Ash says, dragging me closer to him. "Let's get some sleep. It's been a long day."

"Love you, Ava."

"Love you too, Mom." With that, she hangs up the phone, and I give it back to Ash.

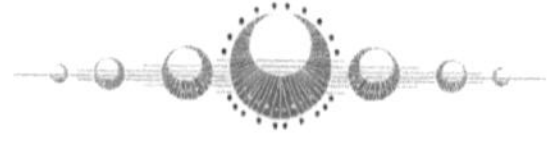

I'm lying in bed fast asleep when my phone rings. I immediately get up, worried it has something to do with Ava.

"It better be the doctor calling us at this time," my wolf groans.

"It better be important," I agree with a yawn.

I stop breathing when I see the name pop up on my screen. Why the fuck is he calling me? Is he looking for Krissy or Dan? Fuck! How am I going to answer his questions without revealing who they were?

I need a game plan. Maybe I'll pretend like I'm on one

of those Spanish telenovelas and act extremely shocked by everything he says.

"Better yet. Don't answer it," my wolf tells me.

I bite my lip until I can taste the warm copper on my tongue.

"Hello," I answer in a sleepy voice.

"Oh great. This again," my wolf says sleepily.

There's no greeting. "Kat, I want shared custody of our kids." I sit up straighter. My breathing stops. Everything becomes so still and silent. As soon as Ash hears who's on the other side of the phone, his body goes rigid next to me.

The grogginess I was feeling mere seconds ago is now gone.

"Fuck no!" Ash says, clearly wide awake now. "He gave up his rights. He didn't want them, and it's strange that he suddenly wants them now," he whispers and rubs his chin in thought.

I'm so shocked watching the scene unfold right in front of my eyes, I forget for a quick second who is on the other side of the phone call. When he says, "Kat," his voice sounds darker somehow. I don't know if it has always been this dark or if this shadow hanging between us is new.

"No."

I pull the phone away from my ear, ready to hang up when he says, "Kat, you can't keep my children away from me. They're mine too." Oh, now they're his too? Where was that attitude when we were signing the divorce papers, or better yet, when he threw us out of the house and cast doubt on the paternity of my kids?

"Yeah, but you didn't want them, remember? You

didn't even think they were yours." I remind him. My voice is stern and confident, leaving no room for confusion.

"Well, now I do." I can only imagine him gripping his phone with white knuckles.

"What's changed?"

"Does it fucking matter, Kat? They're mine." Something isn't sitting right with me. Why would he want them all of a sudden?

Is there a new girlfriend he has and wants to act like a loving father? If so, I don't fucking care. He's too late.

"Go to hell, Theo. You're not getting shit from me." My hands shake as I hang up the phone.

Something is up with Theo; I just can't pinpoint what it is. As much as I want to stay in bed with Katarina and reassure her that Theo can't come here and take the kids, there are other threats that are harming my family.

I leave Katarina's room with a promise of taking her out to dinner later, and I walk straight into Tyler's room, but he's not here. Maybe he's still at the cabin.

I need to burn off this energy. I think about calling Tyler to spar, but I'm in no mood to get my ass kicked. So, I take my wolf out on a run instead.

Once my body is tired, I go to my room and quickly put on a fresh suit and dial Tyler's number.

"Everything okay with Kat?" he asks, sensing my distress through our bond.

"We need to talk. Theo called her three hours ago. Meet me in my office. I'll tell you about it," I say as I walk downstairs.

"I'm on my way," he replies before hanging up.

I go to my desk and pull out a drawer full of paperwork and background checks on Theo. Tyler gave me a full file on him when we were tasked to keep Kat safe. The first time I read through the papers, I was expecting him to be clean, but now, I'm realizing he's way too perfect.

My focus was on Katarina at the time, and because she was our main priority, I may have skimmed over some details about her ex and their kids.

Tyler bursts through the door without knocking. "What's going on, Ash?" He's ready for a fight, and I haven't seen him this wired in a long time.

My wolf's head pokes out of his cave. *"Except when—"*

"Not a word." I stop my wolf from finishing that sentence. It was a fluke anyhow. I could've taken him down.

"I'll tell you when I call the others. I need you to check on Theo's family. Dig up everything you have on him. His story is not adding up."

"I fucking knew it," he responds. "I never leave anything to chance." He'd talked to me about wanting to check further into Theo, but I stopped him, thinking he was being too paranoid. Our only focus at the time was getting Katarina to our property. "I'm going to get dressed and then I'll be right back." I'm just now realizing he looks sweaty. I should have known he went to the gym.

He closes the door behind him as he leaves.

We haven't been able to use our link in so long that I've forgotten we have it now. This will be my first time trying it since we got our powers back. I'm afraid to use it.

"Why?" my wolf questions.

"I don't know. Maybe because I'm afraid that it still won't work. Or I'm afraid that it will work and we'll lose it again." This was our bond. Our right as a pack. And the thought that it could be taken away again terrifies me.

"Krissy was probably the only witch that was able to do that. The only reason she was able to take it from us was because she stole her ancestors' magic," my wolf tries to reassure me.

I sigh. *"You're right."*

"I know I am." Cocky wolf.

With a deep breath, I mentally call for them. *"Az, Benji, come down to the office. I've got some news to share with you."*

"I've missed this," Benji says in a chipper voice inside my head.

"You better not be yapping through our link now that we have it back," Az responds to Benji.

I would normally taunt Az for this, but I'm so focused on the task at hand that I let it go.

Five minutes later, both Az and Benji attempt to stride into my office at the same time, shoulder checking each other at the entrance as they both try to squeeze through the threshold.

"Hey, it's Kat," Az says, looking over his shoulder down the empty hallway. Benji's head jerks back to see around Az, but he's already pushing Benji out of his way.

"You asshole," Benji says as he realizes it was a trick to distract him. Az only chuckles. They take up the two chairs right across from me.

"You couldn't tell us through our link?" Az asks,

already bored and twirling his knife. He senses my unease, and he's being cautious.

I guess I could've, but I'm not used to it yet. "No," I say instead.

"So what's the news?" Benji asks, moving to get comfortable.

"We're waiting for Tyler." As soon as the words leave my lips, Tyler steps in wearing a fresh pair of sweats and a T-shirt.

"We're all here," Tyler says as he leans against the wall.

"Theo called Katarina this morning."

They all look stunned, and if this situation wasn't so serious, I'd laugh at their shocked faces. Their surprise morphs into anger, and in an instant, they are ready to brawl.

"What the fuck!" they all shout at the same time.

Az's hatred turns into a sinister smile like he's ready to play. That's the mode I need him in right now.

"Az, go check on his *family* and take reinforcements. I don't have a good feeling about this."

"We need to make her our alpha female of the pack—our Luna—as soon as possible. We're more vulnerable when we're not presenting as a unit when it's known that she's our mate. Have you been able to talk to her about it yet?" Benji asks hopefully.

I shake my head. "Not yet. She was too tired to discuss anything last night. I'm going to take her out to dinner. I'll tell her then."

"You better, Ash. We don't have the time to wait." Tyler leans his head against the wall like he's building up a plan in his mind. I won't ask him because I won't understand his gibberish talk about hacking and computers.

"Ash, you need to tell her by the end of the week. We've waited a long time." Benji is right. It bothers me that I didn't catch on that Emma was never our mate. I should've known that Emma wasn't it by the way Katarina commanded my attention.

"We need to talk about Ava," Az interrupts. Our heads move in his direction.

"Is she okay?" I ask immediately.

"She was fine when Benji and I left the cabin early this morning," he says as he looks contemplative on how to say the words next.

"She's not . . ." Az looks at each of us trying to figure out how to say it. "I mean I don't think she's like her mom."

"So she doesn't have violet eyes? Maybe that's why she didn't shift?" Tyler asks as Benji pulls out a red apple and bites into it, making a loud crunch.

He shrugs when we all look over at him. "What? I'm hungry."

"I don't know how to explain it. Her eyes were different from ours, and her talons were darker and sharper."

"Fuck," I say, slumping back in my chair.

Benji takes another bite. "Maybe she can't shift at all."

"Even if she can't, we won't kick her out of this pack." Packs are known to kick you out if you can't shift. We've made it known that we run our pack differently.

"We'll work it out with her. When she's better, we can

ask Ava if she'd like to work on shifting, and if it doesn't happen, she doesn't have to worry."

"Isn't it a weird coincidence that as soon as her gift is activated, her father calls." Tyler rubs his chin in thought.

"How would he know about Ava's transition?" Benji asks, taking the last bite of his apple.

"Yeah that's the real question," Az says looking at his phone.

"I'll go over the files. There are pages I have questions about," Tyler says as he walks back to the door.

"I have the address of Theo's parents. I'll pay them a visit," Az says as he gets up from the chair.

They both leave my office.

"Benji, roam the property. I have a strange feeling that there might be someone who isn't supposed to be here. Ask Amara to help you track. If you find anyone, don't kill them. I have questions."

"On it," he says, and he too gets up from the chair and walks out.

Something about Theo isn't adding up. If my theory is correct, then he's a shifter just like us and both kids are going to end up being shifters as well.

I slump in my chair and twirl the ring in my hand. I took it from Katarina's belongings. Can you blame me? I want her to have no part of her ex anymore. Just the thought of him being with Katarina causes jealousy to bubble in the pit of my stomach.

When I hold it up into the light, the ring pulses, and I sit straighter. Something isn't adding up. It's faint, and you can't feel the power, but the vibration of this ring means it's something else—something more.

There was a reason Krissy let her have the ring back, and it wasn't because she didn't want it. She was checking something.

It held Katarina captive.

Theo is definitely not human, that's for sure. But what exact species is he, and why wasn't I able to feel something when he was here? How does he hide it so well? And probably the most important question of all, why doesn't Katarina know?

I fucking knew it!

I knew there was something off about Theo. It was a gut feeling, and I told Ash, but no, he insisted I was wasting my time and we needed to find Krissy. All of my resources had to be spent on her.

Well, now that has come back to bite us in the ass. *"Thanks, Ash,"* my wolf grumbles.

"We should take him out back and beat the shit out of him again." I chuckle and so does my wolf. We don't take life too seriously like we used to—that's Ash's job. Although, I'm not opposed to beating his ass again like I did the week before Kat showed up.

If I wasn't so focused on finding Krissy and using the rest of my time to find information on Kat, I would've found something on Theo sooner. I just hope that we aren't too late or that he's not a danger to us. But calling out of the blue tells me that he might be a problem soon.

I arrive at my warehouse where I store all of my hacking

equipment. It's also the place I use to hide away from people when I just need some time to myself. When I lock it, no one can get in unless I let them.

My place is huge, and I don't have to worry about so many people being crammed here. There's lots of room and space for everyone.

My warehouse also has a gaming room. I have a ping pong table, five different arcade games, and I have video games set up on another side of the room. Comfortable couches and lounge chairs line the walls for when I invite people. My employees work at the five long tables near the front door.

I stop by the glass cabinet where I keep the first computer the guys bought me. It started my love for computers, and I keep it here as a reminder of where it all began. Gazing at it brings back so many memories. It's the first time I felt like I had found something other than physical training and competitions to make me feel complete. The guys gifted it to me years ago, and my life has changed for the better ever since.

I remember Benji would fight me to play Tetris, then I remember the time he tried to store his bombs in here. We got into a huge argument. He lost of course, so he keeps his shit elsewhere. I didn't want to come here one day to unwind and find nothing but a giant crater in the ground. I've spent a lot of time and money getting this place exactly how I want it, so I'll be damned if he blows it up by accident.

Besides being with Kat, this is as close to heaven as I'll ever be.

Our beta, Matt, stands next to my desk.

"We have six other people coming in," he says, glancing down at his phone. I'm actually surprised they're willing to come in on their day off.

Once the supernaturals start trickling in, I move myself to my desk at the front of the room. Some come in with their own equipment and sit at the open tables, others sit in front of the computers I already have set up.

I arrange the projector on the wall and try to prepare myself before I give out the information my people are waiting for.

"Tyler." Carter, another beta, approaches me. The betas know we like to be called by our name and not our title. "They're waiting for your instructions." He dims the lights, and I turn on the projector with a sigh.

"So we're looking for any information on Theo." I bring up a picture of his face. Ash took it when he went to their house to pick up the kids. The man has no photos of himself on his website. It's like he's a ghost.

"This is all we have on him." I show them the next slide with the little bit of information I gathered the day before we went on the lookout for Kat. "We've got to check both human and supernatural databases. If you find anything at all, no matter how small, come find me and let me know."

"Nothing will get past us," Matt says with determination.

"You got that right." I point to him with my pencil. Carter turns the light back on. "Okay everyone, let's get to it."

By evening, we still haven't found anything, and my

frustration is getting the best of me. I can usually find any information in a couple of hours, but it's nearing dinner time, and we still haven't found anything useful.

We've only found the information with his family, his marriage certificate, his law firm, and his school information. I hope Az found something better.

Everything he has on here is too generic, almost as if he's been preparing for someone to look into him. It's too generalized, which wouldn't normally raise any flags, but the only time I met this man, he didn't give me a good vibe. I thought it was jealousy because he was married to the most amazing person, but I'm now realizing it was more than that.

I smile at the memory of his face twisting in rage and disgust when he saw the mark I left on Kat. He has no idea how special she is—he really fucked up.

A phone call pulls me away from my thoughts. I grab my phone from the table. "Hey, man. I need your help," Benji's voice comes through the phone.

"Why didn't you just use our mind link?" I ask, it's probably the same reason I forget to use mine. We aren't used to this anymore.

"First, because I keep forgetting we have it back, and I actually don't want to keep your focus away from your task."

"What's going on?" I sit a little straighter, rubbing my neck. The stress is getting to me.

"There's two men on the property that are not part of our pack or any of our visitors. I need your help with these guys."

"Who the fuck are they then?" my wolf shouts in my head.

"They said their leader told them to report back on Ava." He doesn't need to say anything more.

"On my way," I tell him before hanging up.

I yell out to my guys as I'm leaving. "If you find anything, message me. I'm meeting up with Benji."

"We got you, Tyler," Carter says.

Who are these guys, and what the fuck do they want with Ava?

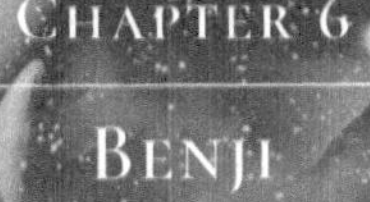

<h1 style="text-align:center">Chapter 6</h1>

<h2 style="text-align:center">Benji</h2>

Hunters.

That one word leaves a sour taste in my mouth. Since I was a young boy, it's been my life's mission to wipe out every single one of them from this earth. Until today, I thought I had succeeded.

Hunters took everything from me—twice—and the memories of my pack, my family, and my baby sister being ripped away from me and killed have fueled my passion for tracking down those bastards and ripping them to shreds. It was the only reason I agreed to join the council to begin with.

Kat mentioned them when I was lying in the hospital bed on the verge of dying. Ash and Az also told me about the hunters, yet I couldn't wrap my head around it until now.

There's no way I can be skeptical while staring at two of them, very alive but closer to death than either of them know.

My guys grabbed them while they were out on patrol. They were trying to hide, but there's no way to mask their scent. They reek of wolfsbane.

The only thing they admitted to was working with a supernatural. I heard rumors when I was young about shifters turning against their own kind, working with hunters to track and kill. After the first attack on my pack, my family had been accused of such atrocities and disowned by what was left of our people. I never thought I would see the day that one of our kind joined forces with hunters, but now I see the rumors are true.

"I guess there's a first for everything," my wolf voices.

"Yeah, I guess so," I agree.

My thoughts are brought back by the two men in front of me grunting. We're at one of our isolated cabins bordering the end of our property where the state forest begins. We don't see humans out this way, so it's the perfect place to hide bodies.

The man to my right has one eye swollen shut, courtesy of our beta, Andrew. The man on the left isn't faring much better. He's got a swollen lip and a broken nose that keeps gushing blood everywhere.

I rest my back against the wall, staring at the two seated men, while Jackson questions them. Andrew is off to the side, his hands clenching, ready to start punching both of them again.

"Who do you work for?" Jackson asks coldly, but he still gets no answer. "What information do you have on Ava?"

The one on the right laughs again. He's already figured

out he's not going to make it out alive. "I'd rather die by your hand than by his." These guys aren't giving us anything. The only reason we know they were looking for Ava is because there was a picture of her in one of the guys' pockets.

I push off the wall with my propped leg and get closer to the men. There's absolutely no fear in their eyes, which only means that they're not lying. The hunters fear whoever sent them here far more than me or my pack.

"Let's show them," my wolf says, and a slow, sinister smile creeps over my face.

It's been a long time since I've called upon my magic. The dark void where my power used to be is no longer there. Now, there's a wealth of energy sitting in its place, waiting to be used. It takes me a couple of tries to get to it like a muscle I have to learn how to use again. Once I do get a hold of it, I know that I'm never letting it go.

"Benji!" Someone in the distance shouts my name, but I'm concentrating too much on what I want to do. The veins in their heads throb, their eyes get wider, and sticky trails of blood track down their faces like tears. They are confused, and when the blood begins to drain from the corners of their mouths, I can see the fear pulsing through them. I watch the crimson puddle beneath their chairs grow wider, and their screams bring me a sick sense of pleasure I can't describe.

"Benji!" There it is again. Someone is not letting me concentrate.

"What the fuck? Leave me alone." My body is calm, and I'm in a trance.

Tyler gets in front of my face, his worried eyes sparking something deep down, and I immediately stop. The two men behind my brother slump forward and sag against the ropes binding them.

They cough roughly, sending a new trail of blood dripping down their lips and onto the floor. Tyler turns around to look at the men.

"You just fried their brains. We can't get any more information on them. I'd expect this from Az and maybe even Ash if they pushed his buttons long enough, but not from you."

I take a step back, and Tyler gazes at me again, his brows etched with concern.

"It just felt so liberating to use our power." I try to explain the feeling to him, to remind him about my personal vendetta against all hunters, but he crosses his arms instead, and I know he doesn't want an excuse for losing control.

The rush of power vibrates through my body, and I think if he could feel this energy coursing through me, he'd remember how powerful we once were.

I want to push him to lose control, to feel the high of our strength. "Tyler, you need to try it and remember how it used to be."

"Yeah, I get what you're saying," he responds dryly.

Does he really, though? It's been one hundred years since we had access to this part of our body. That's a very long time, even for shifters. I forgot what it was like, and I'm sure the others have too.

"You can't let the power go to your head, Benji." The

angry lines on his face melt into concern, and my body sags as the adrenaline fades.

"I need to clear my mind. I'm going to step out for a minute." Tyler moves to the side, letting me go.

I open the front door and walk out. Ash looks up as I close the door behind me, bringing the cigarette in his hand to his lips as he strolls toward me.

"You look like you need a smoke," he says as takes a long drag.

"I just used our power for the first time today." His brows shoot up in surprise.

"How did it go?" he asks. But I have a sneaking suspicion he might already know.

"I basically turned their brains into mush." He watches me like he wants to wring my neck for making that mistake. You can't get information out of a corpse, and losing the hunters so soon leaves Ava in an unknown peril.

"We still need—"

"Yeah, I know," I say, kicking a rock on the ground. "But I can't deny how powerful it made me feel. I . . . I missed it." We started ignoring this part of ourselves like if we didn't talk about it, we'd forget, but this came about when we bonded. It was something special we were given.

He hands me a cigarette, and I take it with quivering hands. When he brings the lighter up, I lean into the flame and take a deep inhale. The rush of nicotine hits my head immediately.

"I can see why you smoke a shit ton of this crap." I exhale. "It sure has a calming effect."

He chuckles, looking down at his feet before looking

up again. "I need it with everything that's been going on lately." He tosses his cigarette butt on the ground and steps on it, and in the same motion, he pulls the pack out of his front pocket and lights another. "What did you find out?"

"They were here when the showdown with Krissy started. They've been running around the property, and I think they know about Ava shifting."

"Shit," Ash says as he looks at the cabin. "Why do you say that?"

"Because of the picture they had in their pocket. I think they've been hiding for maybe a week. Probably when Kat saw that light she told me about that day we went to work. Other than that, they haven't been too forthcoming. I think they're more scared of whoever sent them here." Although, after seeing our power, I'm not so sure if that last part is still true.

"We need to know who sent them," Ash says, twirling his lighter. He looks to be in deep thought.

"Yo, Benji. What the fuck was that?" I'm finally calm enough to not react. I wouldn't like to go head-to-head with Tyler, and I would have done just that with the adrenaline pumping through me moments ago.

"He would have taken us down." Even my wolf knows not to mess with Tyler. We've known since we met at the Academy. That's why I befriended him and stuck by his side.

"I tried our power for the very first time, and I'd forgotten how good it felt to be able to unleash it," I remind him.

"You'll have to be with Az and Ash when they use it. The high of feeling power will no doubt be the same for them."

My wolf doesn't mention Tyler because he doesn't need to. He's too composed to get carried away, unless it's about Kat, then he gets riled up.

"Did you find out anything about Theo?" Ash asks Tyler, who's leaning against the post with his arms crossed.

"Nope." He shakes his head in defeat. "Clean as can be. He checks out, I got Andrew to call the Washington State University of Law School he supposedly attended, and they all vouch for him." I wonder if this information is true—if he really did go to this school.

"He's got to be supernatural, but what exactly is he?" Tyler stares at the floor, rubbing one thumb over his bottom lip in thought.

"That's what I'm hoping Az will find out. I called him a little while ago, and he is checking it out with his colleagues," Ash says as he inhales the last of his cigarette before he throws the butt on the ground and stomps on it.

"Are his colleagues human?" I ask.

"Az said they were," Ash says, moving in closer and lowering his voice.

"But we thought Theo was human too until Ava tried to shift," Tyler mumbles, rolling his eyes. This mistake is clearly getting to him. Tyler wanted to push for information to begin with because he felt something wasn't adding up, but Ash told him to stand down.

"So, what's your point?" Ash asks defensively, picking up on Tyler's attitude.

I'm starting to wonder if we'll have another fight on

our hands. Normally I'd be excited and call Az, but right now, we don't have the time for them to act like kids.

"My point is . . ." Tyler emphasizes. "They could be masking their smell as well."

"I'll have Az trail them to be sure." Ash turns and stalks off, and I'm surprised he didn't start shit with Tyler. He must feel guilty about calling off the background search on Theo.

Tyler watches Az disappear before he turns his hardened stare on me. "Theo is going to bite us in the ass. We need to find out what he is and what he wants before it's too late."

I nod quietly as my wolf scoffs. *"Easier said than done."*

Chapter 7

Az

Something nags in the back of my mind as I stare into the grainy picture of Theo that Ash sent us. *"It's almost as if we've seen this person before."* My wolf paces back and forth trying to remember. Have we truly seen him before?

"Maybe it's just because Ezra looks so much like his father." I find it strange that Ava and Ezra don't have pictures of their dad on their phones—especially considering how many they have of us already.

"Nah, it's something else." I just can't quite place it … yet.

I knew something was off with that piece of shit Kat called a husband. He rubbed me the wrong way. My instincts were right about him. At the time, I hated Kat, so I thought what I felt for Theo was based on resentment for casting his wife out and making her our responsibility somehow.

When he came into our home, he gave me strange

vibes. He looked down his nose at each of us like he was carrying a secret that made him superior to us.

"Mr. Samson is ready to see you, sir." I get up from the chair and walk to the woman sitting at the front desk. She's got brown hair and brown eyes. I've caught her staring at me a couple of times. Maybe the tattoos on my face make her uncomfortable, or maybe she senses my supernatural aura, but whatever it is, this woman can't keep her eyes off of me.

She knocks on the door before she opens it. "Mr. Samson, Az is here."

"Let him in," the man on the other side says. She opens the door wider, and before I step in, she tries to grab my arm to lead me closer into the office, but I pull away quickly.

"I'll be outside if you need anything," she says a little too sweetly. I choose to ignore her weird behavior and drag my eyes to the man sitting behind his desk instead.

I walk up to the man and shake his hand. "Mr. Samson, I'm glad you were able to see me on such short notice." This is the last man Tyler told me to check on. He said it was difficult to find the few people he found. None of us want to ask Kat who Theo hung out with unless we absolutely have to. I think we should just tell her our assumptions on Theo and the others agree, but Ash believes she has too much on her plate.

So instead of building our relationship, we're going for secrecy, really smart of us to go this route," my wolf annoyingly voices his opinion.

I let go of the man's hand and sit down across from

him. "What can I do for you today?" Mr. Samson looks bored like I'm wasting his time. My appearance doesn't help any, but I don't give a fuck about what people think about me.

"I'm here with Business Magazine, and we're interviewing firms to see who to give our next donation of one hundred thousand dollars to." I just spit out the first thing that comes to mind. "We've narrowed it down to five. We're now conducting interviews."

"Interesting. Why haven't I heard of . . ." The man turns to his computer to start typing, and I think he's looking to see if the magazine really exists. I have to ask my questions now before he finds out there's no Business Magazine.

"How long have you known Theo Antonelli?" His fingers freeze on the keyboard.

As soon as I mentioned Theo's name, his face lit up. "About twelve years."

"Is there any information you can give us about him?" I grab a notepad and pen from his desk to try and act like I'm writing this all down, but I doubt the man notices.

"What can I not say about the man?" he chuckles like we're old friends. His demeanor changes. His face softens, his eyes grow glossy, and his shoulders relax. "He's very generous. A really good guy. Always cracks jokes," he says, leaning back in his chair and getting more comfortable. "I was so sad to find he and his wife divorced. They made a beautiful couple." It takes willpower to sit calmly and not slap him for the comment. I'm itching to get my knife out and slice the older man into pieces. But instead, I hold on to the side of the chair and remain somewhat calm.

"Is something wrong?" I may not be as in control as I thought I was.

"Thank you for your time," I say as I get up abruptly and the chair falls to the floor.

"Wait, don't you want to know more?" the man stands up, and his brow lifts in confusion. This man won't give me any information I need.

"I've heard enough." I yank the door open and step out.

My long steps take me further from his office. As I stride past the receptionist, she immediately gets up and hurries right behind me. My hackles rise, preparing for a fight. Is she human or supernatural? Fuck, I'm getting paranoid.

"Sir, can I get you anything?" the woman sounds desperate.

"No."

"Can I have your number?" I immediately stop in front of the double glass doors. Oh, that's what she wanted.

"I'm taken," I say with a small smile and push the door open. I grab my shades from my front pocket, put them on, and walk out of the building.

I checked two other colleagues of Theo's and found absolutely nothing. I think they were glamoured—they have to be. Our conversation was too perfect, and it sounded rehearsed. They made him sound like the most amazing person ever. But when I talk to Kat and the kids, they say otherwise.

"Some people are fake in front of others, and their true colors come out behind closed doors," my wolf says. That's true, but the only people who seem to admire Theo are the ones who speak of him with glazed eyes, and that alone seems questionable.

There is something there I just need to get to the truth of it all.

I get in the car and drive to Kat's old place. As much as I don't want to see the house where Kat was married to someone else, I need to find information on this man.

Twenty minutes later, I'm parking across the street at Theo's house. I should have probably driven something more discreet instead of my cherry-red 1956 Ford Fairlane, but I'm at the point where I don't fucking care if he sees me.

If we find each other, even better. Maybe I'll get to kick his ass for being such a dick to Kat and our kids.

"No one messes with our Luna," my wolf howls.

Hours pass, and I haven't seen a car pull up. No one here pays me any attention. They all believe nothing will happen within the walls of their cookie-cutter homes.

By three in the morning, I kick my seat back a little more and put one hand over my rumbling stomach. I wish I had thought to bring along some leftovers that Lily stashed in our refrigerator because hunting right now is out of the question. I've been sitting here for hours watching the snowfall gather on the roads, and Theo still hasn't shown up. I'm starting to think he doesn't come here anymore. Was this place all for show?

I need to take my precious car back home before the

snow really piles up. If I get stuck, I'll never hear the end of it from the guys.

I get out of the car and tug my jacket around me to block the crisp air. Not that the cold does anything to shifters, but when I'm in public, I try to blend in as much as possible. I look both ways to see if anyone has spotted me. Once I'm sure I'm the only one out here, I stop rubbing my hands together like a human and run across the street.

I stand on the curb facing the house. So, this is where Kat lived most of her life? I never actually made it to the house the night she turned for the first time. We shifted and searched the area where we believed she was bitten. We should've come to see her instead. That will be one of my biggest regrets, that we searched for the man who attacked her instead of coming here and helping her.

I walk around the property to see if I sense any magic. I do two loops, but there isn't any trace of it. My brothers are going to be pissed that I'm searching the property by myself after Ash told me to take reinforcements. Hell, I would be too if one of my brothers did the same. A part of me hopes that I run into Theo out here alone. I want to slice him up and hack him to pieces. The others would just go in for the kill, but I . . . I want to make it hurt.

I stand cautiously at the entrance of the house, looking all around for any signs of Theo. He didn't smell like a supernatural, but there is no other way to explain why Ava is shifting.

I twist the doorknob and find it unlocked. Strange, but

before I think better of it, I push it open and let go of the handle.

I gasp, nearly dropping the knife in my hand but catching it before it falls to the floor.

Everything is gone. It's like no one has ever lived here.

I invite myself in and take silent, careful steps as I walk through the living room, through the dining room, and then into the kitchen. Everything looks spotless. I walk upstairs to the bedrooms, and all of them are perfectly empty.

I linger outside the biggest room of all, and knowing this is where Kat slept makes me angry and territorial. How I wish he were here so I could kill him.

I open the door to the master bedroom, and the place is just like the other rooms in the house. There is nothing to show that a family has lived here.

I don't smell anything. It's like it's been vacant for years instead of months.

So if Theo Antonelli doesn't live here anymore, where the hell is he?

Where the hell are you, Theo?

CHAPTER 8

KAT

I t's the middle of December now, and for the last couple of days, my stomach has been turning like it knows something big is about to happen. I haven't gotten a call from Theo since that early morning when he demanded custody of our kids, and I know he's getting ready for something big. I just don't know what it is.

Theo won't sit there and do nothing, especially when I hung up on him. No, not my ex husband he does whatever the fuck he wants. He always has and always will. He's got friends in high places, so even if I'm supernatural and can cause serious damage, he'll still be protected.

I'm waiting on the edge of my seat for his next move, and I have a feeling I'm not going to like it. It did feel good standing up to him, and I'd probably do it again, but knowing the way that man operates, he doesn't like to lose. He'll hit harder next time, and that's what scares me. I should be preparing, but it's hard when you don't know what to prepare for.

Life has been nothing but chaos since I turned into a wolf, and it's only been a couple months.

It's been a week since my daughter turned into a shifter, and although she hasn't been able to fully turn into a wolf, that's a problem for another time. It's strange to even think about it. Only a few months ago, I thought everyone was a regular human and then . . . *bam*! I get bitten and my whole world changes.

Ava was doing much better when I visited her the next day at the cabin. Her color had returned, and it was like nothing happened to her. She appeared completely fine. Ash assured me it was because she has faster healing abilities now and that it was safe for her to finally come home and get settled back into her normal routine.

I can't help but think about whether or not I'd be scared of her if I wasn't a shifter. I'd like to think I'd be an understanding mom, but the doubt keeps creeping in. In the back of my mind, I wonder how this shit happened or if Ezra is going to go through the same thing.

"Hey, Ava." I walk into her room. She looks chipper sitting on her bed with books, pencils, pens, and binders piled on top of her zebra comforter.

It's hard being a mom of teens. I feel like you can never really know if you're doing a great job. I'm pretty sure it doesn't matter what age you are, you'll always be wondering if you're being a good mom, but throwing the supernatural world into our daily lives has been disruptive. All I know is that I'm doing my best with what life has thrown at me.

"Mom." I look up at Ava who is now in front of me.

Not realizing I've sat in the corner of her bed. She leans over her schoolwork and grabs my hands in both of hers. "This is not your fault. You know that, right?" I want to look away, thinking I'll see disgust in her beautiful face, but instead, I see happiness, and my jaw unclenches.

She squeezes my hand in comfort. "I can't help but feel like this is all my fault . . ." If I hadn't gotten bitten, maybe she wouldn't have turned too. Unless . . . No. It can't be.

"Mom, none of this is your fault. There's nothing you could've done to prevent this. Life has thrown so much shit at us," I want to correct her for cursing, but it seems small compared to all we've been through. "We've survived what life has thrown at us, and we'll do it again. This is not the end for us."

I smile. "Ava, when did you get so philosophical?" She chuckles, gripping my hands tighter.

"I've always been this smart." Heavy footsteps approach the room, and I already know who they belong to.

We both turn our heads and find Ezra leaning against the door.

"Yeah, right. I've got the smart genes from Mom. You come in second."

Ava scoffs, throws him a dirty look, then grins as my younger son walks away. Ava drops my hands and climbs underneath her covers.

Wanting to stay just a little longer, I look around her room. She's added a lot more since we first moved in. There's more art, pictures of her friends, and a small sofa in the corner.

I look down at the book in her hands. "What are you reading?"

She follows my eyes and looks down. "Oh, it's for school. Ryder brought it to me. Apparently I have to study for a test," she says grumpily. "We're having tests all next week. I guess what I just went through is considered normal here and no one is treating me differently."

I shiver at the thought. The first transformation was definitely not normal. "I still don't know why I didn't shift though," she says. The corners of her mouth tighten in sadness.

"Maybe your body was just tired," I offer up.

I think we're all just as puzzled. The guys reassure me that if she doesn't shift, she'll always have a place to stay here. Apparently other packs shun you if you can't turn. That's so devastating to think about.

"Yeah," she sighs. "Az says it might be all the stress. He wants to go out after finals and try to get me to shift."

"Can you feel your wolf in there?" she moves her head to the side in confusion.

"I know that there's something there. I just can't quite grasp it." I want to ask her if her wolf talks to her, but I don't want to disappoint her just in case it doesn't.

"What are you being tested on?" I look down at her book and find that maybe I should read this too. I need to get familiar with the supernatural world if I'm living in it.

"It's about the war between the werewolves and lycans," she says as she looks down at the pages.

"Aren't they the same thing?" They sure as shit don't look the same, but I thought they were all wolves.

"We most definitely aren't." My wolf huffs as if I've just offended her.

She sits up straighter, and her face lights up once again, forgetting her sadness from earlier. "Lycans stand on two legs and are way harder to kill. Silver bullets don't do shit to them."

"Language, mija," I say sternly.

"Oh, sorry, Mom," she says sheepishly. "This history just gets me so excited," she says with glee.

"Are they still alive?" I ask curiously.

"Lycans? Nope. They all died out." Oh wow. Well . . . this turned depressing fast.

"I thought the guys looked big and scary, but this one looks scarier," I say as I stare at the picture in her book. I shiver just looking at those bright red eyes.

"Do we know how they died?" I ask curiously.

"Nope." She looks down at her book again. "All it says is that they died out. I'd like to think it was the werewolves who killed them," she says with so much fierceness, I'm almost taken aback.

Well, I know it's fucked up to say, but at least I won't have another creature trying to kill me. I've had enough supes trying to put me in my grave.

I look at the time. I don't want to keep her up any later. "Well, rest up because you have school after this weekend." It's Thursday night, so she only has a couple more days before she goes back, and by the looks of it, she's going to be tested the whole week before winter break starts.

She closes her book and lays it on her end table. "Yeah, I'm starting to feel it," she yawns, gathering the pile of books from her end table and dragging them over to her desk.

She walks back to her bed and gets under the cover again. "Good night, Mom."

"Good night, mija." I get up and kiss her forehead before leaving.

I go across the hall to check on Ezra. I open the door and glare at him. "Alright, alright, Mom. I'm going to bed, sheesh."

I'm going to kill Tyler for the gaming system and computers that Ezra lives on.

He sees my scowl and turns off all the screens before hopping into bed.

I walk in and give him a kiss on his forehead. "Good night, mijo."

"Good night, Mom."

I close his door and walk back to my room. Another door in the hall clicks shut, and I look back to see that it was Az's room. He still won't talk to me, but he follows me around.

He was gone for three days, and I panicked the entire time, but Benji assured me he was just doing a job. It still didn't stop the nerves from coming right up. I'm thinking it has something to do with us being mates. I crave to be around them all the time, but I don't want to sound like I'm being too needy, so I haven't pushed.

One of my guys sleeps next to me every night, and so far, they've been trading off.

Ash still hasn't talked to me about the night we had sex, and I know none of the others would. They think that

Ash is better at talking about serious shit like this, but he's probably the worst at it.

He's so serious about everything. The night at the brothel was the only time I've seen him let loose, and I thought I was seeing a new side of him the night we had sex —until he tried to kill me.

Once inside of my room, I stare into the mirror with a sigh, focusing on the violet specks in my eyes that have slowly begun to overpower my normal shade of brown.

I tentatively bring my hand to touch the the heart tattoo and gasp.

"Holy fucking shit!" I shout.

I need to go back to the tattoo shop.

It's late, so I won't be going today, but I plan on asking Az to go with me tomorrow. I'm tired of him avoiding me, and maybe the extra time together will give us the chance to resolve our issues.

I get why he's mad at me. We had a moment together, and I've completely disregarded it and his feelings since everything has happened with Ava. I know he gave a lot of himself when we were together, and I really hope he can forgive me for how I've gone about things since.

The next morning, I'm twirling my knife restlessly in bed when her cherry-sweet scent hits me and my body stiffens.

I wait to see if she's going to knock, but I quickly grow impatient . Instead of stomping to the door and ripping it open, I walk to my closet and pull out a drawer to organize my ropes. Keeping my hands busy helps keep my mind busy.

I grab my favorite rope and can't help the way my mind immediately pictures it tightly twisted around Kat's curves. I can't even think about it without getting hard. She hasn't spoken to me since the night I nearly killed her, and I know that I should be the one to approach her, but I'm hurt she has barely been able to look at me.

There's finally a knock on the door, but I don't get up from my position to answer it. She tries the handle, but it's locked.

My cock stiffens at the thought of her wanting to come

into my room. When my phone rings, I pick it up from the floor and watch Kat's name flashing across the screen.

I don't want to answer it, so I continue to arrange my ropes aimlessly to distract myself. On the last ring, I finally give in and pick it up, but I say nothing as her soft sigh fills the line.

"Hey grumpy. I didn't think you were going to answer." My body immediately reacts to her sweet voice, begging for me to open the door and let her through, but I keep my position like the stubborn man I am.

"I wasn't going to, and I'm not *grumpy*," I add, maybe only to convince myself that I'm not.

"Yeah, you are," she says with a small chuckle. I want to open the door and see her beautiful smile in person, and I have to push myself to remain in place. "Well, if you don't want to come with me, I'll just have to go by myself."

My wolf and I sit straighter. There's no way we're letting Kat go anywhere by herself. "Where are you going?" I try not to sound too desperate, but that's exactly how it comes out.

"I'm not telling you that until you open the door." A loud growl comes up from deep in my belly. I know she heard it through the phone, but she doesn't say anything about it.

I grudgingly get up from the floor and walk to the door to open it. Kat's there leaning on the doorway with her phone in hand. The first thing I notice is her cheesy smirk.

She's so damn perfect. I grip the door handle tightly; it gives me something to do when all I want is to fist her hair and put two fingers in between her plump lips.

"Hey, Az," she drawls, and I want to crush my lips to hers, but I stand there and wait. I know I'm being petty, but she hasn't looked for me once. She ran away from me because she didn't trust that I wasn't going to hurt her again.

"This is the first time I've seen you in a long time. Although . . ." She gets closer to me and runs her index finger down the small opening of my red button-up. "I can feel you following me everywhere," she whispers. "You watch me everywhere I go." She's not wrong. I'm not letting her get far if I can help it.

I want to grab her and lock her in my room and keep her here forever. I want to worship her body as I make her bleed. I want to paint the walls with her blood.

"Where are we going?" I ask before I make good on the fantasy in my head.

I don't ask her where *she's* going because I'm going wherever she does. My cold heart is excited that she sought me out specifically.

When I spent three days away from home, my wolf and I missed her so much. I wanted to just give the job to someone else, but I knew that I had to check the information for myself.

"If I can drive your car, I'll let you know." She bounces up and down with a gleam in her eye.

Yeah, there's no way I'm letting her drive my baby.

There's no way in hell she's going to touch the driver's seat of my car, and from the pointed stare I give her, she's well aware of that.

She shrugs. "I had to try."

I grab my keys from my dresser. "Let's go." When I hold her hand, a tingling sensation shoots through my fingertips, and I pull her closer to me, wanting to inhale her cherry scent.

She smiles widely like I just fell into her plans, and I probably did, but at least I get to be with her now.

We get to the garage and she sprints, hauling me along after her.

"A couple rules, Kat." We stop in front of my pretty red car.

She turns around and narrows her eyes, taps her foot on the concrete floor, and shows me just how impatient she is.

"No eating or drinking or sneezing or coughing or . . ."

"Yeah, yeah, yeah. I got it, old man." Now it's my turn to narrow my eyes. "Now open this baby up." I unlock the doors and she immediately opens it and gets in. "Whoa, this is nice!"

She looks around the car in awe.

"I know it is because I paid a pretty penny for this one."

She runs her hand through the interior, and I get a little jealous she's not running her hands along my body.

"You'd probably tie her up and have your way with her before she could touch us," my wolf says as he watches her with joy.

"You're probably right. Maybe I should tie her up after she rubs her hands all over me."

I put the key in the ignition, and she groans when the

car's engine starts up. I have to keep my jaw tightly shut. This is going to be an uncomfortable car ride.

I clear my throat before asking, "Where are we going?"

As she comes back to reality, her cheeks turn slightly pink, which only intrigues me further. Where did her mind go just now? It certainly wasn't where we were headed.

"Oh umm . . ." she scratches her head nervously. "The tattoo shop."

"You're getting a tattoo? We actually don't have to go anywhere because we have tattoo artists here and they're pretty darn good." The truth is, I don't know if I'd be able to watch as another person puts their hands on my girl. I think I would only see red and want to kill the guy. Yeah, this is not the best idea.

"Oh no, I meant the tattoo shop where I got my heart tattoo." She touches tentatively where hers is.

"Why do you want to go out there?" My insecurity is really showing. A pang of jealousy hits me that she may want to see Theo, but then I remember she's mine. She will never escape my clutches; I will never let her go.

She leans in closer to me. "Az." I move my body to the side so she has my full attention. "So, I'm not sure how to explain this," she says nervously. "But I think Jess hid my powers in the heart tattoo." When I don't say anything, she continues. "I know this sounds crazy, but every time I touch it, there's some sort of pulse."

Without thinking, I extend my hand towards her face she leans into my hand. I cup her face and run my thumb over her heart tattoo. I don't feel anything. "I don't think you're crazy. I will never think that of you," I say softly. We sit like this for a few minutes.

My hand falls back to my side. "Let's go find out," I say quickly, silencing my need to undress and fuck her right here.

She enters the address on my phone, and I place it on the dashboard.

As I pull out of the garage and start driving, Kat can't keep her mouth shut like usual. Not that it bothers me; I love listening to her. "Have you . . ."

I wait for her to finish, but she doesn't say anything else. "Have I what?" I say leaving the property.

"Have you, you know . . ."

"Kat, I have no clue what you're getting at."

"Ugh," she groans loudly. "Sometimes I forget how old you guys are and that's why you don't understand *what I'm getting at.*"

"Hey, we're not that old." I look at her and she lifts a brow. "Okay maybe older than you, but by our standards, we're still pretty young."

"Fine whatever." She waves a hand. "Have you fucked in this car?" I nearly stomp the brakes from shock, but I recover quickly.

"Why would you ask that, little brat? Would you be jealous if I had let someone defile my precious car?" she folds her hands and avoids contact with me, opting to stare straight ahead.

The tension is there in her shoulders. We drive onto the freeway and start our three-hour drive. I let her stew for a couple of seconds because I like seeing this jealousy in her.

Knowing that she reciprocates these possessive feelings for me is everything.

"The answer to that, brat, is no. I haven't fucked anyone in this car." The corners of her lips twitch.

"Good, it would suck if I had to track down that bitch and claim my man." I'm stunned by her words. Is my little brat wild just like me?

She talks through the whole ride. She's a talker just like Benji, but I'd rather hear her voice than Benji's any day. Benji just talks about shit I don't care to hear, but with Kat, anything she says sounds really important to me.

She's quiet for a couple minutes as if she's contemplating something. "There's something about classic cars that makes me so horny, Az." I tighten my hands on the steering wheel. She brings her hands down to her lap and starts rubbing her thighs. "I don't know exactly what it is, but I've always dreamed of getting fucked in one."

I clear my throat. "Little brat, what are you doing? You're playing a dangerous game." My voice is hoarse and full of need. I've had her once, and I want to taste her again. She's the perfect drug, so addicting and alluring.

She pulls her tits out from her V shirt and starts to play with her nipples. My cock is hard and getting nearly uncomfortable sitting in this position.

"Sir," she moans. I turn to look at her briefly, and she bites her lip. Fuck, she's going to be the end of me. "Can we fuck?"

My breathing quickens and she takes off her seatbelt. "Little brat, put your seatbelt back on," I tell her sternly.

But she doesn't listen and crawls across the leather bench seat to the driver's side.

She unbuttons my pants, pulls the zipper down, and slowly pulls out my hard dick. I glance down from the road just a moment to see her warm tongue shooting out and grazing my piercing. All I want to do is close my eyes, but I keep my focus on the road ahead.

I move my hips forward, giving her more access, and she greedily takes it in her mouth. "Fuck little brat what are you doing to me?" I growl.

It's getting harder to concentrate on the road. The next exit I'm getting the fuck out of here.

With one hand on the wheel, I use the other one to push her head further down my cock. I grab her hair, using it to push and pull. She chokes on it but keeps lapping every inch of me.

After taking the next exit, I find an alleyway and park. "So, you want to play?" I say darkly as I yank her violet strands and bring her face close to mine. "Then we'll play," I tell her as I drag her out of the car, still fisting her hair.

I may have taken on more than I can chew.

Az's eyes look darker somehow. I'm not afraid . . . Well, maybe I'm just a little afraid. When it comes to Az everything is unexpected.

"Alright little brat, strip for me." My jaw drops to the floor, and I look around the building on both sides knowing that anyone can just walk by.

"Az, right here?" I ask, surely he doesn't want me naked out in the open where people can see us.

"Yes, right here, and it's sir to you. You know what will happen if you don't call me that?" I know exactly what will happen. He'll bring the flogger down on my ass.

It's December, and the air is colder, but it doesn't bother me anymore. I hesitate, looking all around as I start to take off my shirt, very aware of the fact I'm not wearing a bra. My tits spring free, and Az lets out a low groan.

Lifting only my ass off the seat, I drag my pants down around my knees and then kick them off into the floorboard. When I finally glance his way, I notice he's still fully clothed in his dark red and black suit, and his arms are locked across his chest.

"Yeah, those too." Az points to my undies, and I look at him again with uncertainty, but he's very serious. I take them off, and as soon as I do, I feel so bare, which is exactly what he wants. Sure, being a wolf has made me accept my body more, but it's still a little daunting to be out in the open like this.

The cold breeze runs over my body, and although it doesn't make me shiver like it used to, my nipples still harden in response.

"Now, get out of the car," he nods to the dim alley in front of us, and I swallow hard. It's almost afternoon, and though most people are probably still at work, it's still very possible that anyone could walk down this alley and have a clear view of what's about to happen. "Now, little brat. I want you on the hood of the car while I get what I need. Don't make me ask you again."

"Yes, sir." I hesitate but push the door open and climb out of the vehicle slowly. My heart races erratically as I walk around the front of the car.

I lean back against the hood of his car and watch the opening of the alley with equal parts fear and excitement. A minute later, Az shows up with ropes. "All the way up," he commands, and I silently slide up onto the hood, hoping like hell I won't dent it. He grabs my right hand and ties it to one of the mirrors mounted on the far side of the hood and quickly moves to do the same with my left.

He circles the front of the car with a pensive look on

his face. When he gets to my legs, he grabs each ankle and positions my bare feet flat on top of the hood.

Exposed.

That's what I am right now. I'm completely naked while he's fully clothed. My pussy and my tits are bare for anyone to see.

I'm more exhilarated than ever. My slick runs down to my ass. "This is perfect, you look so fucking flawless." He takes his phone out and takes a few pictures. Even if I wanted to, I can't cover myself up, and I'm not sure if I even want to. "I want to remember this moment," he says before putting his phone back in his pocket.

He gets close to my body and lowers his head. I can't bend my elbows to look. I can only lie here and take whatever he unleashes on me as I stare up at the sky.

He runs his talons across my legs and warm liquid spills from the wounds he created. He licks the cut from my leg before he stands up and leans his body close to mine. His lips are red with my blood, and if I wasn't already horny, that sight would have gotten me there.

He runs his nails under my breast, spilling more, and he laps it all up. I moan loudly, not caring anymore if it brings an audience. He runs his talons through the peak of my nipples, and I gasp at how sensitive they feel.

"Do you remember your colors, little brat?"

I nod my head, but he doesn't like the way I respond. "Answer me," he growls.

"Yes, sir," I choke out.

He leans back, and I can't see what he's doing. All I know is that one second, he's pulling something from his pocket, and the next there's a cold piece of metal against my ass. I squirm a little, but his harsh tone stops me. "Don't move." I try to relax my body. "It's for your ass so that you can take my dick there."

He runs the toy up and down my entrance before pushing it further in. I've never gotten fucked here before, and I'm a little nervous about it, but I trust Az, and I know he'll make it pleasurable.

"I missed you, brat," he says as he pushes the butt plug in and out. "You didn't seek me out. I thought we had a moment." There's a hint of sadness in his voice, and I wish I could see his expression, but he's facing down and focusing on what he's doing.

"We did, sir." I gasp as he pumps the toy in and out. "I didn't know how to come talk to you." He steps back finally, leaving the toy in and my bottom feeling so full.

"I told you this ass was mine, and now I'm going to take it." He pinches my nipple before he runs his fingers through my folds. "Little brat you didn't lie when you said you were turned on, did you?"

"No, sir."

"Is this why you wanted to fuck in my precious car, defile it like no one has ever before?"

"Yes, sir." As those words leave my mouth, he hovers over my pussy before he sticks out his tongue and licks it clean.

I look up at the sky as he ravishes and sucks on my pussy. I try to contain my screams. There are apartments on both sides of the alley with windows open. I have no clue if people are watching us right now.

I wish I could hold on to something but my wrists are all tied up. I'm whimpering when I feel the release starting to build in my stomach. I curl my toes on top of his hood and try to contain my loud screams. When I finally come, I bite my lip so hard that the blood pours over my tongue.

I'm panting hard. He stands up looking satisfied, and I watch as he runs his tongue slowly down his bottom lip to taste me.

"Little brat, if you keep looking at me like that, I'm going to shove my cock inside of you with no warning." My breathing gets harder thinking about his pierced cock being inside of my dripping pussy.

"Now for your ass." I squeeze tighter but he still manages to get the toy. I don't know what it says about me, but I'm missing the loss of it. He chuckles darkly. "You liked it didn't you?"

I think about lying but he'd know. I purse my lips together before answering, "Yes, sir."

He goes back to the car and opens it and then closes it. "Lift your hips up." I do as he says, and he slides the blanket beneath my back. I'm higher up this way.

He grabs a bottle of lube from his pocket. For someone that says he's never had sex in his car before, he's really prepared.

"You're overthinking," he says, watching my expression. "I've seen the way you look at my car, and I might be a little over prepared, but I've been dreaming about this day too."

"I better be the one and only that you fuck on this

car . . ." I have no idea where those words came from. He lifts his tattooed brow up. "Sir."

"That's better." I strain my neck downward to see what he's doing. I watch as he pours a good amount of lube and rubs it up and down his tattooed shaft. He finally brings his pants down just a little bit to have his cock exposed, and my mouth waters.

He grabs both of my legs and sets them down on his shoulder. "Only for you little brat, no one else."

He aligns his cock with my ass and slowly starts to push in. There's pain around the rim, and I have to gasp. I must have shut my eyes because he says, "Open them and look at me." His tone is so demanding that I have to do what he says. He pushes in slowly and carefully.

"Sir, I don't know if I can fit anymore of you back there." It's true, I think . . .

He gets closer to my face and brings his mouth to mine, but it's not something passionate. It's hungry and demanding, just the way he is. I take a sharp breath and my head falls back against the car.

I look down and notice the streaks of blood across my breast. These cuts are deeper than the ones before. He pushes his cock the rest of the way in while rubbing the blood all over my breasts and lower abdomen.

He thrusts while he rubs the blood all over my tits, his tattooed hand bringing it to my neck and gripping my throat. "You're mine," he says with so much possessiveness that it startles me.

I can't reply because he's holding me so tightly that the

tips of his talons puncture my neck. I can only imagine what this looks like to outsiders.

"Hot fucking sex," my wolf says.

He lets go of my throat and brings it back to my pussy. He draws circles on my nub, bringing me to an orgasm. I scream so fucking loud, no longer ashamed. I'm sure people on the next street heard.

When it hits me, his erection expands, and he thrusts a few more times before pumping his seed into me. "Now you're going to carry my seed the whole ride there and back."

I'm too exhausted to respond. He gets off and reaches over to untie his knots from my wrist. He's quick. He leans his body over mine, and I take a moment to admire the tattoos peeking out from the neckline of his suit.

He gets off me, and I hear him in the trunk. He comes back with two towels, which only means there's a lot of blood. He wipes me down, and my body is too exhausted to move. But fuck if that wasn't sexy as shit. I hear a few people talking, but I pay them no attention.

Az brings my clothes and helps me get dressed. Once I'm done, he carries me to the passenger side. "Fuck Az, that was some intense shit." His body stills for a minute, and I look at him. Is he nervous? "But I loved it, and I want to do this again," I add quickly. He lets go of a breath. I guess he was anxious.

He hands me a water bottle after sliding me back into the car. "Drink, Kat, you need to hydrate." I take it from him, open the cap, and pour the cold liquid down my throat. Once I'm done, I hand it back to him.

He walks over to the driver's side and gets in.

This time I'm too tired to form words. The drive to the tattoo shop is quiet, but we're both satisfied. My ass aches, but in a good way. Now I'm imagining having two cocks in me at the same time.

I look around and sit up straighter when I notice we're no longer on the freeway. Az pulls up to the shopping center where the tattoo shop is. My heart pounds rapidly. Az reaches over with his tattooed hand and grabs mine, trying to soothe me.

These people should know what to do with my heart tattoo. Right?

Az parks and I get out of the car quickly. He holds out his hand, and I grab it, ignoring the ache in my back side. As we approach the building, the dim storefront sends a wave of disappointment through me. The tattoo shop is closed, and not just closed for the day, it's permanently closed.

What the hell am I going to do now?

<h2 style="text-align:center">Chapter 11</h2>

<h2 style="text-align:center">Kat</h2>

I'm standing here with my mouth wide open, not realizing that Az just picked the lock. "Come on Kat." He waves his right hand my way, trying to get my attention. But I'm focused on the closed sign on the window.

He grabs my hand and pulls me through the door of the dark shop.

"It looks like it's been closed for a while," he whispers for my benefit. I think he's trying not to spook me, but it's already too late for that. The energy in this place doesn't feel quite right.

My heart sinks, and I want to cry out in frustration. Why does this shit keep happening to me? Can I catch a break for once?

The whole place is deserted. The two couches that sit near the window are turned upside down. The cushions on the chairs are ripped down the middle with the white pad coming out. The glass from the piercing display cabinet litters the floor, and every step I take makes a loud crunch as I try to tiptoe through the mess. If anyone is here, I'm sure they can hear me.

"Let them come for us," my wolf shouts in my head.

I take a moment to stop and glance around the area. It's as if someone tore the store apart while they were looking for something. I wonder if they found whatever it was. Unlike me, I can't seem to find the answers to my questions. It seems like every day the unanswered questions keep piling up.

The only people that might have known what really happened with my tattoo are gone. I'm starting to get frustrated by all of the dead ends.

I touch my cheek, and the tattoo is pulsing against my fingertips. I can feel that it wants me to find a way to set it free.

I watch Az looking around the room, twirling his knife between his fingers. I'm not sure what exactly he's searching for. His training makes him look so lethal. He always seems ready for anything.

He looks up at the ceiling, and I follow his gaze to a camera. The red dot is blinking brightly. How did I miss that?

"It's time to go, Kat," he says, as he grabs my hand and we walk out of the tattoo shop. My body shivers at the thought of being watched and not knowing who it is.

"Who do you think is on the other side of that camera?" I ask Az.

"I don't know, but I'm not getting a good feeling about this."

You and me both.

My body tenses, waiting for someone to attack.

His eyes roam around the shop like someone is going to appear out of thin air. I almost laugh at where my mind takes me, but I sober up once I realize that might be a huge possibility. After all, I don't know every supernatural there is, and appearing out of nowhere could be a probability.

"I need to get you out of here before someone tries to come after us. I'll have to let Tyler know to hack into this camera." Having Tyler being a computer nerd is a huge asset.

"Yeah, my creep-o-meter is going up." The hair on the back of my neck stands, and my eyesight changes as my wolf takes over.

Az opens the door, and we rush into his car. He puts the key into the ignition, and we high tail it out of here.

My heartbeat starts to slow down as I take a much-needed deep breath. I almost feel bad for making Az come all the way here for nothing, but then I remember what we did on the hood of his car, so I can't say I really regret it too much.

"Do you remember what the tattoo artist looked like?" he asks as he turns right, heading to the freeway.

I shake my head before answering, "No, I was too drunk to remember." I only recall it was this place because Jess mentioned it once, and I looked it up because I wanted another tattoo, but in the end, I chickened out, or maybe it was Theo's influence after all.

"Jess died with my secrets, and now there's no one for

me to ask. No one for me to go to for answers." I stare out the window longingly.

"We'll figure out a way, Kat. We always do." There is no doubt in his voice. He'll go to the ends of the world to figure out a way I can remove this heart if that's truly what I want, and it is. I need to know if this is what's truly stopping me from being able to use my powers.

"Do you think this can be taken off with laser surgery?" I ask hopeful.

"The heart is a tattoo but it holds magic. It can't be removed the human way." My hopes deflate once again but I'm committed to finding a way.

Three hours later we make it back home. I'm tired but my body keeps vibrating with adrenaline. I don't know if it was the sex I had with Az earlier or if it's because I'm determined to figure out a way to remove the heart, but my mind is on go-mode despite my body aching for sleep.

I go to the bathroom and take off my shirt. I look at myself in the mirror and see the red stains on my skin. The remnants of what Az and I did. I never thought I'd let someone control my body this way, but I loved it. I love giving myself to my mate.

I take the rest of my clothes off and step into the shower. All the red runs off my skin, tinting the water pink as it spins around the drain and disappears.

Once I'm done, I go back to my bedroom and stare at my tattoo. The tattoo was the craziest and most exhilarating thing I had ever done in my life at the time, but now, it's a reminder that this is hiding who I truly am. The people who did this to me thought I was so dangerous it was best to keep it a secret—even from myself. I was led to believe I was human my whole existence.

I wonder if this somehow keeps Ava from shifting. If I'm somehow causing her not to be able to shift. Maybe she's not even a shifter at all and she's what I am and I'm causing her harm because my magic has been locked up. It's a scary thought to think that I may be the cause of her distress.

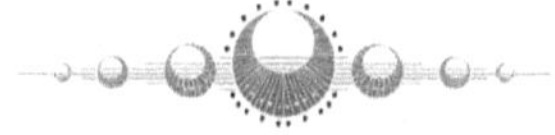

The next day, I eat breakfast at the dining table with my family, and I try to suppress the anxiety creeping into my every thought. Something is going to happen soon. I feel it deep in my bones. Either with my magic, Ava, or Theo. I don't know what it is yet, but I spend the entire day spacing out.

I'm so deep in thought that I don't hear Tyler until I bump into him. "Oh sorry, Tyler."

"You okay, Kat?" His features are etched with concern as he grabs my shoulders to steady me.

I think about lying and telling him that I'm completely fine, but he'll just see right through it. Plus, I hate when Ava tells me everything is fine when it isn't. It's not fair to do it to someone else.

"I-I-uh, I don't know." Although I want to be truthful, I'm not sure how to explain what is going on right now. "I'm just feeling a little unsettled."

"About?" he pries.

"I can almost feel something big coming, and I'm not sure what it is, and it scares me." His face softens.

"Whatever it is, Kat, we'll be ready." He sounds as sure as Az did.

I nod and force a smile. "I'm going to rest before my shift tonight." He reluctantly lets me go, but not before giving me a kiss on the forehead.

I go to my room and stare at the tattoo before lying on the bed and drifting off to sleep.

Evening comes, and I'm nearly ready for work. "Almost done," I call out to Benji when I sense him by the door.

"I'm playing tonight." Since I've watched him play for the first time, he's been practicing his songs in my room sometimes. He tries to finish a full song, but that never happens. Right in the middle of it, I always end up on top of him, and he moves his guitar to the side of the bed while I'm ripping his shirt off trying to get to his bare chest.

Benji gets a look and winks, already knowing where my mind wanders.

"Now I know how you get Kitty Kat," he says knowing well how much my body craves him. "But we'll have an audience at the Crescent Lounge." I grab my lipstick and face my vanity table. I can watch his reflection through the mirror, and my eyes flick over to him. "I want you to know that I don't give a fuck who's watching. If you want to fuck me then go ahead." He smirks. Well, that wasn't what I was expecting.

I chuckle. "Benji, I don't know how I'll be able to contain myself." I slump on my chair dramatically using my hand to fan myself. "Every time I hear your voice, all I want to do is take my clothes off," I say sarcastically.

"I have that effect on women." He shrugs nonchalantly.

"There will be no sex in front of everybody." Ash comes into my room. "Az was too careless when you guys did it in the alley, and so were you Benji." He folds his arms and leans against the door.

Ash, as handsome as he looks, reminds me of an old man. "You're such a prude, old man." Benji goes to my mirror and fixes his hair.

"Aren't you guys the same age?" I ask. Last time I checked, they were all equally as old.

"We are, but I don't act that way." Benji faces me with a look of mock hurt that makes me laugh.

Ash throws his arms up in the air and waves them in exasperation before leaving the room.

After work, I'm completely beat. The kids are hanging out with their friends and the guys are downstairs in the kitchen talking about the possibility of how they can remove the heart from my face. I'm too tired to weigh in on the conversation, so I go upstairs to my bed instead.

I grab a paranormal, why-choose romance book about dragons by Dreia Wells, and when I can no longer pry my eyes open, I drift off to sleep, not waiting up to see who sleeps next to me tonight.

I'm woken up by the feeling that someone is watching me. I try to control my breathing, but it becomes harsher. I think of my dagger that I keep under my pillow, and my hand creeps up slowly until my fingertips wrap around the handle.

How did the guys not notice someone breaking in? Thoughts of being kidnapped again run through my head. No, there's no way I'll let anyone take me again.

Fisting my weapon, I sit up abruptly, only to find a man with platinum blonde hair staring at me.

"Fuck, Ash! Why you gotta stand there all creepy and shit?" I let out a long breath to ease my anxiety.

He clears his throat. "Sorry, didn't mean to scare you."

"Well, you did a shit job," I say, putting my weapon back under my pillow. Since there's no threat, I don't want to accidentally stab anyone.

I run my hands over my face, already feeling sleepy again.

"Ash what time is it?" I yawn.

"It's five in the morning." Gah, It's so early for a weekend. I worked late last night and stayed up longer than anticipated reading my book.

"I'm going back to bed, are you getting in?" It doesn't feel awkward to ask him to come to bed. Hanging out with my men seems so natural now that it feels kind of silly that we disliked each other when we first met.

"Actually, I wanted to see if you wanted to go to breakfast?" he asks, but I've already laid my head down on the plush pillow. I pull the covers over my face before answering.

"Yeah, give me like four hours and we'll go," I mumble.

"Come on, Katarina." I can almost hear the pout in his voice. He's probably upset right now that he can't make me do anything that I don't want to—even if he is an alpha.

"Ugh fine. I keep forgetting you're all old men that like to do things extra fucking early."

Once he leaves, I go back to sleep.

He didn't say what time I needed to be ready, so I take that as a win.

Two fucking hours.

That's how long it took before Katarina showed up in my office. By now I could've just cooked breakfast and eaten it or went out hunting.

"You didn't tell her when she needed to be ready," my wolf gently reminds me. He's been so smitten with her since we found her.

I sigh. *"Fine."* Next time I'll just have to be clear, but Katarina will do what she wants anyway; that's what I love about her.

Well, I must say Katarina looks hot. I have to adjust my pants so my cock isn't so visible. I can't think with my dick right now. We've got an important conversation coming up.

She's wearing a red plaid winter dress with black leggings and a pair of tall black high-heeled boots. My mind slowly starts to wander through images of undressing her so she can stand in front of my bed naked with just those boots on.

I shake my head to clear my mind. *Focus Ash,* I tell myself.

Just for the hell of it, I narrow my eyes on her. "Katarina, really?" I grab my pen and twirl it around my fingers while I lean back in my chair.

She stands by the door with her hands on her hips, ready to chew me out. "Ash, you didn't tell me when you wanted me ready or what I needed to wear." I stand up as she rambles on defiantly.

I grab her arms and pull her closer to me. She yelps in surprise, and before she can speak another word, I crush my mouth to hers. She tenses for a moment like she wants to argue with me some more but finally gives in.

She pulls away from me, breathing heavily. Her arousal and mine take over the room.

"What was that for?" she asks as she uses her thumb to wipe her lipstick off my lips.

I go to the front of my desk and lean on it. Katarina follows me, she hikes up her dress to her thighs. That's when I notice the garter straps holding the lace top. I guess they weren't leggings at all. She gets one knee on the surface of the desk and then the other one. I grip her ass while holding her close to me. She grabs onto my shoulders for support.

Her pussy hovers over my cock. When my length starts to twitch, a clear sign that I want her riding me, she moves her body back and forth to create friction.

Fuck eating, I'll just have her instead.

"I thought you were going out for breakfast?" Benji interrupts, closing the door behind him. She looks back at my brother with need. Benji grabs her violet hair and crushes his lips to hers. She moans in his mouth before they pull apart. "Good morning to you, Kitty Kat."

Benji hikes up her dress until her lace thong is showing, and his fingers disappear behind the purple fabric. He rubs her heat in small, leisurely movements, and she groans against my ear.

"We should go," I say through gritted teeth, but her sweet smell is everywhere. The last thing I want to do is leave. "We can come back home, and I could please you endlessly."

"No. I don't want to go anywhere," she whines. "We can eat later." Her breath increases with need.

"He's right," Benji says, taking his hand back and helping her adjust her dress so we no longer see her drenched pussy. He knows we've got important things to discuss, and as much as I want to keep her here and pleasure her, we've got business to take care of first.

She pouts but brings her shaking legs to the floor and stands. She smooths down her dress, and Benji whispers in her ear, "I'll be here later if Ash over there can't satisfy you." I punch him hard on his shoulder. He lets go of Katarina. "I'm kidding." But to Katarina he murmurs, "Well, mostly." He winks at her before running out the door before I get another chance to hit him.

"Let's go," I tell her, not at all grumpy.

We walk out of the office and to the car, and we both get in. "Ash, I love the way you fuck me." That startles me, but I can't help myself. My chest puffs out feeling good about myself. We've only had sex once when she was on her cycle and we haven't done it since. I've been too chicken shit to go for it again.

"I hope we do it again soon." She grabs the seat belt and buckles herself in. I'm too stunned to move.

"Well, if that wasn't a sign, I don't know what is," my wolf says. *"Tell her something about how much you enjoyed it,"* he urges, and I should already know better than to listen to my wolf about trying to make awkward conversation with Katarina.

"Yeah, that was fun," I say, and she snorts like she found my response funny.

"Oh no . . . I already see how disastrous this will be," my wolf moans and rubs his eyes with his paws as if he's embarrassed by me. *"I'm going back to my cave. I can't watch this anymore."*

"I'm not that bad." I try to defend my human side.

"Yes, you are." He walks back into his cave, shaking his head, leaving me alone with Katarina.

We park in front of the restaurant. "Oh good, there's almost no one here." This is what I was hoping for so that Katarina and I wouldn't have any distractions. Usually, my people like to come up to me and have a chat about concerns or what they like about something or just regular chit-chatter, but right now, my head is not in the right space to talk to my pack.

"It's like eight in the morning." She yawns. "Who in their right mind would be up so early on the weekend to go eat breakfast?" She takes off her seatbelt and glares at me like she wanted to stay in bed longer.

I purposely avoid her eyes and get out of the car. It's not that early, I tell myself. The sky is just starting to lighten up.

"Hi, Ash. Hi, Kat." We're greeted by one of the hosts, who is a pack member. "Would you like an indoor or outdoor seat?"

"Outdoor please," I tell him. I look around the area, and the few people who are here nod our way, lowering their eyes as a sign of respect. Katarina just smiles at them brightly. I'm not sure she even knows that they did it out of respect for both of us.

I bend down and whisper in her ear, "They're trying to be polite."

"I know, but it's still weird. I don't want to be treated any differently." I stand back up, but not before I kiss her exposed neck. That's exactly how the guys and I like to be treated. In my travels a long time ago, there were alphas who would make their pack leave if they were in a restaurant. I always thought it was fucked up. Some would also make their people look down when they were speaking to them. My brothers and I rule differently. We hate the old ways of pack living and vowed to never be one of those assholes.

"Come this way." The host grabs two menus and leads us outside. There's no one but us here. Just the way I want it.

Our bodies regulate our temperature so we don't feel cold, but they still have pyramid patio warmers, but they only turn them on for other supernaturals who can't regulate their temperature like we can.

"Your server will be here soon," he says politely as he drops the menus on the table.

We sit down across from each other and pick up our menus.

"Everything looks so delicious," she says as her stomach starts to grumble.

She narrows her eyes at me, already knowing I have something smart to say to that, but she's lucky we get interrupted.

"Good morning." Our server sounds chipper. He's probably been up for a while, or he's just really excited that we're both here. "Are you ready to order?" He flips our mugs over on the table and pours two steaming cups of coffee.

Katarina immediately grabs hers and inhales the aroma before taking a sip. "It's so good," she mumbles. "It's exactly what I needed." Maybe she won't be so upset anymore.

"If you had lured me out of bed with coffee, I probably would have gotten up earlier."

I take a drink of mine and savor the taste. She's right, it's like a cup of heaven. Maybe all I needed for her to be in a good mood was to bring her a steaming cup of coffee. I'll make sure I do that before waking her up so early next time on a weekend. On weekdays, her internal clock wakes her up early. She's groggy and sometimes grumpy, but she still wakes, and it doesn't take her two hours to get ready like it did today. I wonder if she fell back asleep.

She puts her cup down and looks at our server. "I'll have the meat and cheese omelet with hash browns, toast, and an order of pancakes on the side." Her face beams as she tells him her order.

"I'll have the same." I close my menu and we both hand it to him.

She rubs the finger where the ring used to be. "What have we found out about Krissy?"

"Nothing yet," I respond before silencing my phone. If it's important, the guys can use our mind connection. We still don't use it often; we're so used to using our phones that we forget. "We're working on it," I assure her. With everything that's been going on, I don't want her to think that we've forgotten.

"I have a feeling deep down in the pit of my stomach that everything will get worse, almost like everything we've been through is preparing us for what's to come." She picks up her coffee and takes another drink.

I know what she means. The guys and I have discussed this. Tyler said she was distracted yesterday. I asked Benji, but work was so busy she didn't have the time to sit and really think about anything.

I know there's a threat looming over our heads. We have no clue what will happen next, and we hate being in the dark so much.

"Have you guys found out anything about the woman with violet eyes? The one who's locked up." She sounds as though it doesn't matter too much, but her heartbeat picks up. She wants to know more than she lets on. She's probably afraid to have high hopes that the lady would have any information that would help her figure out who she is, and she's convinced herself it doesn't really matter.

"Nothing yet, but we're on it, Katarina." She nods her head sadly. I don't like that look on her. It feels like we're failing her, but that's not what I want at all.

Fifteen minutes later, our server brings our food, and her face lights up with happiness. She drenches her pancakes in syrup as she takes a bite of her omelet.

She's devouring her food, no longer counting carbs in her head. What a relief to break her of that habit. I hate how she thought she had to keep herself skinny. I fucking hate Theo for making her feel as if she needed to lose weight.

We're having a lovely time. I watch her eat, and I've barely touched my food. "Ash, are you going to eat?" She points at my untouched food.

We haven't bickered once since we fucked. Knowing that I need to bring this conversation up makes my stomach churn.

I just need to come out and say it, but when I open my mouth, my wolf makes an appearance. "Katarina, is Theo a supernatural?" She drops her fork, and it hits the plate with a loud noise that I'm sure everyone inside the restaurant heard.

She looks at me with dread in her wide eyes. I've just brought her whole world crumbling down.

She leans back, crossing her arms before answering, "What . . . what do you mean?" Her cheerful voice is now gone, and I hate that I had to bring this up. I wish we could go back to me watching her devour everything on her plate, but we need to know because if Theo is, then he's more dangerous than we thought and we'll need to prepare.

I push my wolf back from wanting to shift. I can feel him vibrating with anger as soon as I mention Theo and supernatural in the same sentence.

"He's not a human." I try a different approach. Maybe she didn't understand the wording the first time.

"*Oh goddess no.*" My wolf shakes its head. "*I'm going back to my cave if you won't let me take over.*" In my mind, he's running as fast as he can to avoid the situation. *Fucking wolf.*

Her brows lift almost to her hairline, and she grabs her coffee and takes another drink to think through my words.

"We believe he might be a shifter, but we aren't sure," I add and she spits out her drink. She grabs the napkins and wipes her dress.

Once she's done, she looks at me again. "I've lived with him for sixteen years, that man is no wolf."

"Was it . . ." I clear my throat trying to think of my next words. This is not easy, and I don't know if it'll trigger other feelings. "Was it maybe a possibility he was hiding it from you?" She opens her mouth to speak—most likely to argue the situation. "It would explain why Ava is trying to transition into a wolf, and it would explain why he wants to see them now after he said he wanted nothing to do with the kids."

She chews on her nail and really thinks about it. "Ash, it would make sense, but . . ." She takes a drink of her coffee, almost like she's trying to hide behind her cup. "But there would have been a slip up." She sounds so sure of her answer. I want to remind her that she wasn't aware he was sleeping around until a couple months ago, but that would hurt her too much, so I stay silent instead.

"You're probably right," I say, trying to end the conversation before I upset her further. Theo is a testy subject for all of us. My brothers and I because we want to murder the person who hurt our mate. Katarina because of all the abuse she went through and not to mention the kids.

"Ash, stop," she says suddenly.

"What?" I adjust my tie, giving me something to do. "What the hell did I do?"

"You're trying to agree with me because you don't want to hurt my feelings. You should know I'm stronger than that."

"As your . . . uhh . . ."

"Mate . . ." she finishes off. I don't want to frighten her again. "Ash! I know what we are, I'm not going to get scared. I also know that I'm the Luna of the pack." At my startled expression she continues. "I had to ask around after Joseph called me *Luna*."

I rub my forehead. This isn't going so well, but I try again. "As your mate, it's in my nature to want to take care of you." And I already know what she's thinking. "And yeah, I know I was a douche before, but I didn't know you were my mate." She leans forward on the table with her elbows propped up. "I was only an ass because I felt like I was betraying Emma."

Her face softens. "Well, as kind as your gesture is, don't fucking sugarcoat it. I want to know the truth. I want to be a part of your secrets, which I know you're still keeping from me." She leans back again, crossing her arms. How do I tell her about the one that's keeping my brothers and me up all night? I have to be sure before I say anything that can be damaging to our new relationship.

I sigh, wondering how she's going to take this next part, but I know it's not fair to keep information from her—especially when it's about her kids. "Az went to check on Theo. His family isn't checking out. Tyler is checking all his records, and they're—just too clean. Whether you want to believe it or not, he's supernatural."

"So . . ." She puts her head down thinking the information through. "Ezra might become a supernatural too?"

"Yeah, we think so." I slump back in my chair, folding my arms across my chest.

"Did Ava have violet eyes?" I hesitate and pray she doesn't ask more because I don't want to lie, but we're not ready to tell her the truth.

"She did . . . No she didn't." *But they're something different.* She doesn't ask about my slight hiccup. I'm not really lying to her, I'm just not telling her the whole truth.

She rubs her ring finger where her wedding band rested, and I try not to show how much I'm jealous of the fact that she notices something missing there.

After a moment she continues. "I thought supernaturals can smell other supernaturals."

"We can, but for some reason, we couldn't tell when Theo and Dante came to our home." The moment the words *our home* leave my lips, my heart skips a beat. I love the sound of that. Kat belongs to us as much as we belong to her. "No, let me rephrase. With Dante, we know his scent was masked because of Krissy, but with Theo, we have no fucking clue." There's something I've been holding in my chest that I need to get out. "Katarina, the next time I see your ex-husband, I can't promise that I'll be civil. I want to shred that man into pieces." She laughs like this is amusing to her, but she says nothing about it. The way her eyes flash to violet is confirmation enough that her wolf wants a piece of him too.

She touches the bridge of her nose as she thinks over our conversation. "I wonder if Dan knew Theo was supernatural, and I wonder if Jess knew Theo was one too." I tilt my head in confusion. "Oh um . . . I sort of forgot to tell you guys that there was a note hidden on Jess's body when we went to visit her." She chokes up, thinking about her dead friend. She clears her throat before continuing. "The note said she knew about Dan, and she had something important she wanted to tell me, but I'm guessing she got killed before she was able to write it down." Her voice is full of sorrow. "There have been so many people in my life keeping secrets. I'm grateful you told me, Ash," she says sincerely, and I almost tell her, but I bite the inside of my lips to keep them tightly shut.

I grab her hand from the table and give it a squeeze, letting her know she's not alone.

She sighs. "I wish I knew more, but he was closed off about his family. We'd rarely go out to see them." She brings the conversation back to Theo.

"Well, whoever he had as *parents* were definitely fakes." I internally cringe for being so blunt.

"Well fuck," she says, pulling her hand away from me,

and I find myself missing the warmth. She finishes the last of her food.

Before my nerves get the best of me, I spill out, "So remember that day we had sex."

It's like a fog has been lifted and she smirks. "How could I forget?"

"Well, what happened with us is . . ." I clear my throat, "is knotting."

"Ah," she says as if she understands the whole reason I brought her to breakfast. "This is the conversation you were trying to have the night it all went down." Her eyes glaze over as if she's not here for the moment. I've probably brought back memories from that day. She shivers and focuses on me again.

"You were tired," I tell her, hoping she understands that I didn't want to necessarily keep anything from her.

"It was a long day, Ash." She sounds tired again, she's probably reliving that whole day.

"It only happens with mates. I thought this was going to be a harder conversation, but you already know what we are to each other." This part might be a little more difficult. "You said it yourself, things for the future are uncertain. The only way for us to be strong as a pack is to . . . mate and form our bond."

"So, what does that entail?"

"A full-blown orgy."

Her cheeks redden and the only thing she says is, "Oh," as she looks down at her empty plate.

"There's one more thing." Her eyes immediately gaze

over mine. Fuck, I don't know how to say this. She's going to kill me.

"So . . ."

"Just spit it out, Ash."

"When the knotting happens when you are on your cycle . . ." fuck my palms are sweaty. I try to use my pants to get the sweat off.

"Ash!" she yells.

"Sorry, it's just that I'm just really nervous, but I want you to know that at the time, I didn't know you were my mate."

I take a drink of my coffee before finally saying, "That's how shifters get a female pregnant." Her jaw drops to the floor, and her eyes widen in shock.

Chapter 13

Kat

After breakfast we drive back home, and I'm not sure whether to be terrified or excited about having an orgy, and I don't know what to think about a possible pregnancy.

"Wolf." She purposely ignores me, acting like she's sleeping. *"Why didn't you warn me about the knotting?"* I wait a minute and still get nothing.

What I'm concerned about is sealing a bond. It's more than marriage, it's a long-time commitment. I wasn't sure I'd do something like this again.

"Was the marriage even real?" she asks, opening one eye.

"Oh, there you are, wolf," I spit, but she closes her eyes again and resumes her pose. She only came out to bash me. *"Here I thought you were ignoring me."*

Yep . . . I get nothing again.

My wolf brings up a good point. Were we even married? I never truly spoke with his so-called parents.

Come to think of it, he bears no resemblance to them at all, but none of that matters anymore. I push it from my mind, not giving it another thought.

Ash parks the car in the front and leaves the engine on while we both get out. A male I've seen before gets in the car and starts to drive off. "He's going to park it." I roll my eyes. Rich people can't even be bothered to park their own vehicles.

I walk two steps ahead of him, but he grabs my hand and pulls me back.

"Are you ready to finish what you started?" he murmurs in my ear. My heartbeat picks up with excitement as he brings me to his room. I'm going to enjoy Ash.

It's so meticulous in here, not one thing out of place. To be honest, I'm kind of shocked that he's willing to have sex in his room. I thought for sure he'd want to go somewhere else besides his sanctuary.

"It's because he loves us." That warms my heart.

"I'm going to devour this pussy," he says as he drops me on his bed and my tits bounce slightly. His eyes change, zeroing in on my chest, and I get chills throughout my body.

I know what's it's like to fuck Tyler, Benji, and even Az, but I'm not really sure about Ash's style. The day I had my period, he liked playing cat and mouse, but I'm not sure if my heat made him act that way.

The nerves are getting the best of me. I just need to go with the flow and do less thinking and more doing.

"What's your safe word when you're with Az?" My heart thumps so loudly, I know he can hear it too. I think he wants me on edge because he sniffs the air. I look down at his cock, straining against his pants.

I don't notice when I gravitate toward the bottom half of his body. I move only when he pushes my head up to face him with one long finger. "Not yet, baby." The way he is so sure, so confident in himself, I can't do anything but listen to him.

He moves his hand from my chin and uses his thumb to smear my lipstick. "You're very beautiful, Katarina." His voice is deep and seductive. I know my cheeks redden at his compliment. It's confirmed when I look past him to the giant mirror he has against the wall.

He hikes up my dress and immediately goes straight to my thong. As he moves his fingers into my aching core, moisture pools between my legs. I thrust back and forth trying to create more friction as his fingers rub leisurely over my nub.

"I said not yet," he says more forcefully this time.

I narrow my eyes and want to tell him to fuck off, but I can't. I want this, and I want him.

"Now answer me, or there will be punishment." I gasp, not expecting this side of him at all. I guess I shouldn't be surprised. He's always shown an air of authority. He likes control and for everything to be in order. You can tell by the way he keeps his office and his bedroom. "Now, I'm going to ask you one more time, and I hate repeating myself, but I'll do it just this once. What is your safe word?"

He lets go of my lips, letting me answer. "We use the traffic signal."

"Hmm . . ." he ponders. Maybe he's thinking about switching it, but then he responds, "We'll use that too." I'm starting to lose concentration as he's making lazy, drawn-out circles on my pussy. "I like it rough, do you, Kat?" He rakes his free hand through my violet hair, waiting patiently for me to answer.

"I like it both ways," I respond, looking up at him. He's holding back, like he's ready to undress me, but he's still playing with me.

"The night we fucked . . ." He has a faraway look, reminiscing about the excitement of that day. "I loved the game we played. Did you like it too?" His Adam's apple bobs as he swallows.

"I did." I remember my body full of excitement from the chase, from wanting to hide and be found, and for the reward that came after.

He pushes my thong to the side and runs his fingers slowly up and down my slit. I lean my head against his chest and moan as he continues his movements at a slow and lazy pace.

"Damn baby girl, you're already so wet for me." The way he speaks turns me on even more, and I didn't know I could be more turned on then I already am.

"Ash . . ." I fist his shirt, on the verge of coming. Those slow strokes are building up. My core tightens ready for my release.

"Shhh . . . I know, baby. I know." He lets go of my dress, and I pick it up before it falls all the way down.

He uses that hand to press his thumb past my lips. "I can't wait to have my cock between your smeared lips."

He's messing up my perfect make up, and yet I don't care. All I want is to pleasure him.

"You're going to take every inch of me, and when I expand, you'll swallow every drop I spill." I whimper against his finger wanting to feel him inside of me.

"Come for me, baby girl," he whispers in my ear, and it's as if he commanded my body, and I no longer have control over it. I scream, my orgasm explodes, and my legs shake coming down from that high. I lean against his chest, my body still trembling.

"Good baby, now it's my turn," he says with a gleam in his eye. He slowly unbuttons his black button-up. My eager eyes take in all of his beautiful upper body and his wolf tattoo. He stops, and I look up at him as he gives me a devilish smile. He's putting on a show for me. He unbuckles his pants slowly, and I almost want to go to him and help him, but he finally takes them off, along with his boxers. His dick springs free, and my mouth waters.

I try to take off my dress, but he stops me, grabbing both my hands and putting them on my sides. "No," he tells me. "I'll do it, now lift up your arms." I do as he says.

He runs his hand across my lacy, violet bra and traces the center of my body until he reaches my thong. He kisses the sides of my tit, his breath giving me goosebumps all over my body. He wraps his arms around me, unclasps my bra, and lets it slide down my arms as my breasts fall free.

Suddenly, he grabs me by the neck, squeezing the air from me, but I know he's in control. Instead of being scared, I'm excited.

"You're going to get on your knees, part those pretty

little lips, and I'm going to fuck that mouth of yours. I can't wait to watch you cry and mess up that perfect makeup you put on just for me." If I wasn't already drenched, his words would have gotten me there.

He lets go, and I inhale deeply as I get off the bed and immediately get on my knees. He pulls my chin, and I open. He looks down at me proudly, running his hand up and down his thick shaft before he slides it into my mouth.

I close my eyes, enjoying the movement as he grabs my hair and says, "Open, baby girl." My eyes fly open, and I watch as he comes undone just using my mouth.

It's a slow pace, just like when he was rubbing my clit. "Ready, baby girl?" That's the only warning I get before he picks up his pace. He hits the back of my throat while he fists my hair. He uses my head to help him thrust back and forth in rapid movements.

I can hardly breathe around his thick cock choking me, and tears stream down my face. He lets go of my hair to wipe my cheeks, but there's no point, the tears keep spilling down my face. "That's what I like to see, baby girl. Cry for me."

Just when I think I can't take it anymore, his dick expands. I shake my head to try and tell him that I can't, but my mouth is too full. I want to tell Ash to stop and let me breathe, but I can't, and more tears stream down my face. He's relentless.

"Look at your pretty makeup. It's ruined now." I can feel him hitting the back of my throat. "The eyeliner and mascara you had on has smeared." I try to pull back, but he fists my head even harder. "Relax, baby girl, it's almost over." I do as he says, my breathing comes out easier, and I moan, loving the way his thick dick feels. "You look so pretty, Katarina," he says as beads of cum shoot down the back of my throat, and all I can do is swallow.

He pulls out, my throat is raw, but the satisfied look he's giving me, makes it all worth it. "We can't have you wasting my cum, can we?" He swipes the drips from the sides of my lips and smears it all over my mouth. "There we go, Katarina. I want you to take in every drop of me."

I sit on my ass, exhausted.

"Oh, baby girl." The sound of that wicked voice of his makes me look in his direction. "Are you tired?" he asks as he bends down on his legs and caresses my cheek so softly with his hands. "We're just getting started."

"Lay on the bed," he commands, and I do what he says. I get up on shaky legs and hold on to my elbow to steady myself.

I lay on the center of the bed as he unhooks my garter straps and takes off my thigh-high stockings. He rips off my thong and throws it to the side of the bed. I'm completely naked, and the way he's looking at me like I'm the sexist woman in the world thrills me.

"Open wider." He slaps my thighs, pulling them apart. He lowers his head in between my legs and runs his tongue up and down my pussy. I close my eyes and can't help but moan loudly. I move my hands, looking for something to grab and fist another cock. My eyes open wide as Az leans against the side of the bed.

"Look at what I have," Az whispers as I pump his length, paying extra attention to his piercing.

My eyes are drawn to his hand. He brings the heart-shaped jewel close to my face. "Ash is going to put it in and get your ass to open up. Once you're ready, Ash will take your ass while I take that sweet pussy." He looks down at where Ash is lapping my juices. Az grabs the bottle of lube from the side table, opens it, and squeezes a good amount onto the plug.

Az hands Ash the butt plug, and without missing a beat, he grabs it. My body tenses up, waiting for the intrusion. "Relax, baby girl," Ash says quietly, running the toy up and down my opening.

Az grabs a couple pillows and stacks them together. "I heard you gave Ash good head just a couple minutes ago." How the fuck does he know that? I never saw them talk. Ash has been with me the whole time. Did I lose track of time or something?

Az grabs my face and lines his cock up with my mouth, his precum glistening down his tattoo and piercing. "You like sucking cock, don't you, little brat?" he asks low and deep. My words aren't functioning.

When Az shoves his cock past my lips, that's when Ash pushes the butt plug in. Instead of screaming in pain, I moan in pleasure, wanting more. He thrusts the toy back and forth while I can feel Az's piercing tickling my throat.

"Did you cry for Ash?" Az asks, grabbing my hair and using it as leverage to push deeper. I nod my head as tears stream down my face.

"Fuck Ash, you're right. She does look pretty like this." He talks to Ash like I'm not even here. Like I'm only a toy for their enjoyment, but I don't mind it at all.

With his other hand, Az's claws come out, and he slashes down my throat until I feel the warm liquid spilling down my chest. I'm almost terrified Ash is going to lose his shit, but he surprises me by saying, "That color looks good on you, Katarina." His voice is husky.

Az rubs the spilled blood across my face, letting it mix with my tears and smeared makeup.

I thrust against Ash's face while he plays with the toy in my ass. I try to pull out Az's cock from my mouth, try to grab him with my hand, but before I come anywhere close, he pins one of my hands and then the other on top of my head. With his free hand, he runs his fingers down my tits, coating them in blood.

Fuck this feels so good. Az's dick expands while Ash picks up his pace, licking my clit and hitting the spot that is going to throw me over the edge. Hot seed sprays down my throat, and I come loudly, but it's muffled by Az's cock.

Ash leaves his dick inside of me, but my body is exhausted. "Little brat, don't you want both of us to fuck you at the same time?" My body begs for it, and my exhaustion clears as I think about taking them both.

Ash lifts me while Az takes my position on the bed. I must have shown how shocked I am that he's willing to be at the bottom. He chuckles darkly and looks up. I follow his eyes, and I see a hook mount attached to the ceiling.

Ash throws Az a red rope. "Hands," he says, and I push my hands forward. He ties them up quickly, then with the other end, he stands on the bed while he ties it to the hoop attached to the ceiling.

Ash's dark sheets have drops of red staining the

comforter. "Open your legs, little brat." I do as I'm told, and Az runs his bloodied finger down my opening. "Color?"

"Green." My voice is raw from deep throating both men.

Az positions himself between my thighs and lines his cock up with my opening. He hovers over my pussy, and when I try to lower myself, Ash grabs my neck from behind. "Not yet, baby girl. First, I need to take the plug out." He grabs the toy, and once it's fully out, I miss it. "You like that, don't you?" Ash murmurs in my ear while he rubs my backside. I hear a bottle opening and then closing, and I know he's lubing up his shaft. He widens my ass and I inhale sharply.

"Focus on me, brat," Az says as he rubs my clit. There's an intrusion in my back side and a small, sharp pain. His cock is bigger than the toy. He starts thrusting slowly, and I look up at my tied hands and moan.

"I don't ever want this to end," I say out loud, enjoying the sensation.

"It won't," Az assures me. Ash pushes my hips down and my pussy swallows Az's cock and fuck me, this feels to damn good.

Az pinches my nipples hard and runs his fingers down my breast, making a big gash. Warm liquid pours out, and Ash rubs it across my nipples. "You look so fucking sexy right now." My whole body tightens with his words.

"More," I choke out.

Az gives Ash a chilling smile, and they find a rhythm that puts us all over the edge. Ash's cock swells behind me, while Az grips me tightly. His bulge starts to get bigger, and I know it's doing that knot thing that Ash had done. He stops thrusting as his dick holds us in place. Az grunts as his seed spills into me, and my release comes crashing down. Ash does one final thrust, screaming my name.

I try to slump forward, but I'm held by the ropes. Ash pulls out first, and I miss the feeling of him inside me. Az keeps me there a while longer.

"I can bask in your scent all day." That's the last thing he says before he raises my thighs and pulls out of me. He stands on the bed and reaches the rope above my head. When he unties it from the hoop, my body slumps forward, but Ash is already there to catch me and lay me down slowly.

My eyes are heavy, so I let them flutter closed, not even waiting for Az to untie me. Ash carries me to the bathroom. I'm so exhausted that I can barely keep my head up as they clean me. Once I'm clean and back in bed, Ash tucks me into his blankets, and I go right to sleep, not even caring that it's only mid-afternoon.

"What do you mean they took Ava and Ezra?" I'm startled awake hearing my kids' names and Tyler's urgency. I haven't even processed the whole conversation fully.

My drowsiness diminishes, replaced by anxiety. Ash is leaning against the door wearing sweats, but Az is gone.

Ever since I became a shifter, it seems as if everyone is trying to kidnap us. We can't catch a break. "This time, I know it wasn't Dan, but who else could have done it?" I fucking watched him die—unless he somehow came back from the dead. Wait . . . is that possible? Can that really happen? Oh God, I hope not. The last thing I need is a fucking zombie of Dan running around.

"No, he didn't come back from the dead," Ash says.

Did I say that out loud? Or can they hear my thoughts?

"You're like an open book," he clarifies. Oh, well I guess that makes sense.

"That's what I'm going to find out, Kat." Tyler walks into Ash's room and immediately envelops me in a hug. "I promise you, sweetheart, I will find whoever took your kids, and we'll destroy them together." He grabs my hands fiercely, letting me know not to doubt him.

"Do we know how they were taken?"

"The kids weren't on the property. They went out to the mall. There were two guards with the kids but they were taken down before they grabbed Ezra and Ava," Tyler answers, rubbing my back.

The anxiety they must be feeling right now. I should've known the threat wasn't permanently gone. I should have kept them here.

"Was the person supernatural?" If they are then it's going to be harder for us to track them, at least in my opinion.

"We aren't sure yet. I'm going to look at the footage and find out. I just came here to let you know what's going on."

I appreciate that, but it does nothing to settle my mind. I should have been stricter and kept them here.

"You can't keep them from going out. How did you like being locked up here?" Fuck! My wolf has a point.

I lean away from his hands and Tyler drops them. "Give me a minute to think." I say calmly because I don't want them to follow me.

I get out of the comfy sheets and walk out of the room, leaving the men behind.

I stand in my room facing the mirror. My eyes look dull

and empty—except for the specks of violet trying to shine through. The burst of power is trying to get out, but whatever spell is in this tattoo won't let it.

"What do you think, wolf? If my powers can somehow help get my kids back, shouldn't I risk it?" I ask her because she has an opinion on this. If I die, we both die. My wolf doesn't know what I am. I have no doubt that she would have told me by now if she knew. These powers were born within me. It didn't come to me because of a bite.

This is how I know for certain that whoever took my kids was supernatural. They may even know who I am. Why else would they take two teenage kids if not to get to me? According to Benji, hunters died out, but we encountered them a few weeks back.

I heard Az and Ash talking to the others; the hunters were after me. So, whoever this person is might be after me too. I can't just wait for them to knock on my door. I need to go to them.

"But what happens if it ends up killing us? Then there'll be no way for us to rescue and protect our kids." She paces back and forth restlessly like she wants to tear something apart. Maybe I should let her out and blow off some steam, but the human side that needs to be in control wins.

It's a hard decision to make, and if we choose wrong, we die. *"The kids should be our priority."* My wolf's voice trembles in my mind; she's just as scared. It's weird hearing her voice quiver in my head. Normally she's so sure and confident of herself. *"I don't know if we should take the chance. It's too dangerous."*

"I don't think we have another choice," I tell her as I sit

down on the edge of my bed. I rub my hands over my face in frustration. *"How did this fucking happen—again!"*

I feel like a failed mother. It's one thing after another, and I can't seem to catch a break.

That's the moment we know we'll do it because even if I die, I know my guys will take care of them like their own. There is no doubt in my mind about that. If there is a sliver of a chance that I can have my full powers and they can somehow help me with my kids, I'm taking it. It may be foolish, it may be reckless, but what choice do I have? I'm not going to sit and wait for them to do something to my kids.

"I'm with you," my wolf says bravely, trying to support this decision. But there's no denying it, she's just as afraid.

I stare at my purse sitting on top of the dresser for a moment before I get up from the bed and grab it.

For the first time, my hand shakes as I grab the dagger. I pull it out slowly and hold it in front of me, taking a long breath.

My nerves are getting the best of me. The possibility that this might cause my death is what's making me stall. But if there's a slight chance of releasing my power or finally being the person that I am meant to be, then I have to do this.

The sharp tip comes out, the whole dagger glowing purple. I exhale as I look at myself in the mirror. I touch my heart tattoo. It's been there for as long as Jess and I have been friends. Now that I think of it, that's usually the time wolves start shifting. I wonder if she was always waiting for this moment—the moment to be able to hide my power.

"It's a strong possibility," my wolf says, standing straight and not moving an inch.

I grab my weapon, putting it against my soft skin, I close my eyes and barely touch the tattoo when it starts to burn.

"Fuck this is going to hurt." My wolf squints her eyes, preparing for the impact, but she's not scared anymore. She's hopeful that we're making the right decision. Hopeful to finally let that side of me come out.

With shaky hands, I push my hair back, and with the other, I slice through my skin. The smell of burning skin makes me want to gag, and the pain is so excruciating that I see stars. Oh God, this is a bad idea, probably the worst one I've ever had.

My wolf howls in pain, I can hear it in my head. I may be screaming or howling, but the guys won't be able to hear me since the doors are soundproof.

I pant harder as tears stream down my face. I try to keep my hands still, but they're shaking rapidly. I look in the mirror as smoke comes out of the blade.

"This can't be normal," my wolf says, trying to recall if we ever saw smoke coming out of this blade when we killed other supernaturals.

I sear through half of the heart. I can feel the magic of the tattoo warring with my inner power. It's like they're both trying to fight for dominance, and my poor body is taking the hit. My face feels like it's been hit a hundred times.

When did I get on my knees?

The power that's in me is trying to fight back. Whoever

did this must have been a powerful supernatural. My head pounds as the markings fights with both the blade and my power.

For my kids. I repeat it over and over like a mantra until I finish. The symbols slice off, and I gag. When I can no longer take the pain, my body blacks out.

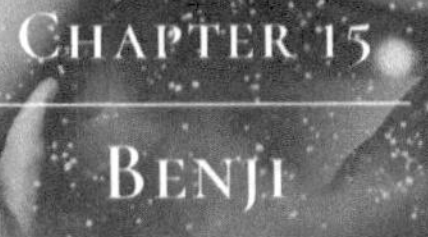

After Kat took off to her room and slammed the door, we made our way to the office to get to work. I don't know how long we've been here brainstorming about how to find the kids and who could have taken them, but I'm surprised Kat hasn't burst in making demands by now. Kat should be in on our plans, but she needs time to think on her own. I can't imagine what she's going through right now.

"I want the security guards who were supposed to be with the kids. There has to be something we're missing—" Az stops pacing the office and braces his hands against the desk. A moment later, a rush of panic hits me. Our eyes meet in question, but Tyler breaks the silence.

"What the fuck is that?" He's clutching his chest, and I think all of my brothers feel the same insane rush of anxiety that's making my heart race inexplicably.

Ash makes the connection first. "Something's wrong

with Kat, that has to be it." He takes off toward the office door and down the hall, all of us falling in behind him. Our bond isn't sealed yet, but there is just something in my gut that's telling me he's right.

We race upstairs. The smell of blood and burnt flesh permeates the hallway. I'm worried she's harmed herself because we failed her, and instantly I feel guilty about not being able to protect her or the kids. The memory of my parents and sister comes to mind; I wasn't able to protect them either, and the thought only fuels me to run faster.

I twist her doorknob, but it's locked, so I kick the door with everything I've got, even though I know that our doors are made of steel.

"Fucking Kat," Az says as he rushes into his bedroom.

"Where are you going?" Ash asks, but Az ignores him, and thirty seconds later, he comes out with his lock-pick kit. We move aside to let him through.

He uses two metal tools and moves them around the lock until it clicks and the doorknob twists open.

As we push through the door, time seems to stop, and the air in my lungs turns rancid.

She's on the floor next to her dresser, loosely gripping her blood-covered dagger, but she's so still.

We're too late.

My heart races as I take in her limp form, and I can see the wheels turning in my brother's head. The confusion, the pain, and the sorrow.

Ash braces himself in the doorway with a sick look on his face, but Az rushes past him and falls to his knees next to her. He pulls her wrist into his lap and digs his fingers into her skin, looking for a pulse. "She's alive," he shouts, dropping her hand.

Those are the sweetest words I have ever heard. She's going to make it. Her own dagger didn't kill her. My body sags with relief.

Her weapon should kill every supernatural it comes into contact with, but it's interesting that she seems to be the exception. Her dagger saved her from the magic that was locked up in the tattoo she tried to sear from her cheek.

"Oh, Katarina," Ash says with so much emotion as he moves from the door and bends down next to Az and Tyler. "She sliced her skin to remove the heart tattoo."

Az shakes his head and gently strokes her hair away from the wound. "She told me she felt a pulse of power. When we couldn't find anyone at the tattoo shop, I didn't think she'd go through such extreme measures to try and get it off. I told her I was going to look into it, which I have, but I came up empty every time. This magic isn't like the tattoo that demons use to hide their true form."

I try not to cringe. The smell of burning flesh is still in the air. It must have hurt her tremendously if she fainted.

Ash shoves Az aside and begins to shake her so she'll wake up. He's gentle at first, but when she doesn't respond, the rattle becomes harder and faster. Tyler pulls him back to let Az take over again, and Tyler calls Amara while I message Doc to have them come in and check on our mate.

Maybe they can help us and figure out a way to get her to respond.

That's when her eyes snap open and relief floods me before it quickly turns into shock and anger.

"How could she be so reckless?" She should've had one of us with her. Of course, we would have all said no to her as soon as she opened her mouth about using her dagger.

"That's probably why she didn't ask," my wolf voices.

"Yeah. You're right," I tell him. The others and I would have never let her do that to herself.

Once our initial surprise is over, we realize she looks fatigued.

I'm standing over her as she brings her shaky hand up and sets it on the wound. She flinches when it comes into contact with her cheek.

"Katarina." Ash's voice is low and full of tension. "What in the fuck were you thinking?" Her eyes widen slightly like she's realizing she fucked up.

"You could have died," I say, crossing my arms.

"What would your kids have said when we saved them and had to tell them their mother died?" Tyler shoves his hands in his pockets, and I can tell he needs to let off some steam. Az has quietly retreated to the safety of the back of the room, but he probably wants to take her to his room and punish her. I wouldn't be opposed to seeing that.

We ask more questions, but she responds to none. "Is it gone?"

Ash throws his arms up in irritation. "That's the first thing you ask?"

She closes her eyes, and when they open back up, we all gasp. She sits up immediately, startled at our reaction. What the hell?

"What? What?" she shouts and looks around her room as if ready to fight.

Az's footsteps come closer. He's drawn to it, just as we all are.

"Your eyes, Kat," Tyler says, his hands tightening into fists at his sides. "They're a deep violet."

"Go," Ash tells Tyler. I know he needs some time to himself because I can feel his strong emotions bursting through our bond. He's not very good at accepting failure. In all the years I've known him, Tyler has been a perfectionist, and when he gets like this, he needs space to work through it or he'll end up taking it out on one of us.

Nothing could get past him when we worked for the council, but now it seems like we're failing at every turn. We haven't found out who took the kids, we didn't know Theo was a supernatural, and we have no idea why Ava can't fully shift.

When Tyler leaves the room, Ash brings Kat to sit on the edge of her bed, while I grab the rag to wipe her face. Her eyes track my every move carefully, and I try to be as gentle as possible, yet she still flinches at the contact.

Forty minutes later, she stands up slowly but keeps drifting in and out. Az picks her up and takes her downstairs to get her to eat something.

I pull out the chair at the head of the dining table so that he can gently place her down. Ash and Az sit next to her, and I sit next to Ash.

I'm happy to watch her inhale the sandwich we made. She has color again, but those eyes still haven't returned to brown. I wonder if they ever will.

"We need to find them." She keeps repeating herself over and over again.

"We will," Az reassures her every time. It's nice to see this side of my brother. He has a hard exterior, but he's just a big softy.

Az looks me dead in the eyes. "Benji, whatever you are fucking thinking about, stop."

"Not a chance," I smirk.

"From now on, you'll always have one of us by your side. We don't know what threat is out there." Ash is thinking of all the worst-case scenarios.

"We know who the threat is," she says more forcefully than I'm used to. "It's fucking Theo. I know it's him." She brings her fist down on the table, rattling the plate. "He has the resources to get what he wants; he always has and always will."

"No I don't—" I start to respond gently.

"Actually, she's right," Az interrupts.

"What do you mean?" Ash asks, looking pensive.

"Krissy masked Theo's scent. Dante had no fucking clue about Theo, but Krissy did. They . . ." He looks at Kat with guilt. "They had a relationship together. She was helping him. I can't quite figure out why. I would like to say that she was in love with Theo, but when Krissy killed her whole family, she sacrificed the love she was able to give and receive for power."

"It makes sense." Kat has a faraway look like she's trying to put all the pieces together.

"Who the hell is Theo, and why is there absolutely nothing about him?" Kat shivers at my question. I can't imagine what she's feeling right now. Her kids are gone, her ex-husband—if we can even call him a *husband*—is not the person she thought he was.

Kat shakes her head before bringing her violet eyes to meet mine. "That's the question I've been pondering. There's something he's keeping from the whole world, something that he doesn't want anyone to know."

e fucked up. Not only did we fail to protect our mate from nearly slicing her face off and almost dying, but we couldn't keep our kids safe from being kidnapped.

I can hear the guys lecturing Kat as I let her bedroom door swing shut behind me. I have so much pent-up anger that I had to get out of there before I said or did something I would regret.

It seems like every time things are going good, something else happens to ruin our happiness.

I head to my warehouse, and as I get closer to the building, I tilt my head up, sniffing to see if there'll be other supes inside, but the smells are faint. Looks like everyone has left for the evening. I walk to my desk, grateful that I'm the only one here. I'm not looking for an audience to see me break down.

I pace around my office for a good fifteen minutes to

try and figure out a plan, but I've got nothing. I can't stop thinking about my girl lying on the floor like a corpse.

Thinking back to the mall's security footage I tapped into, it was obvious that the people who kidnapped Ava and Ezra were hunters. But not the hunters we're used to. These hunters left the other wolves unharmed.

"Hey, Tyler." Zay comes into the warehouse, and I turn around to face him. "Did we find out anything new?" I had Benji tell them they were hunters because they've been on edge about finding out who took Ava and Ezra.

"Nothing new yet," I tell him, and his shoulders sag in defeat. "Try and get some sleep. You'll be of better use if you're rested." He nods his head and steps out.

I finally take a seat, grab my phone from my front pocket, and dial Silas's number. "Hello, Tyler." I can smell his deep arrogance through the phone, and I grip my phone tighter.

"Silas, you better not be fucking with us, or I swear, I'll fucking use our power and destroy you once and for all."

"I'd love to see that happen," my wolf growls.

"Me too, wolf, me too," I respond.

"As humorous as that would be to watch you *try* . . ." I hate this cocky bastard. "I have no idea what the hell you're talking about."

"I'm not here to play games, and I don't have time for stupid politics. I need answers, and I need them now. My mate's kids, who are now mine too, are gone." I feel like shit, and I can't find anything in my security to help me track them. "Hunters took them," I say through clenched teeth. It's really hard for me to accept defeat. I've never been one to accept it.

The job they did was clean—too clean. They were in and out. Ezra and Ava were both in different locations, but according to the mall cameras, they were taken at the same time. Ezra disappeared when he went into the arcade with Ryder and Cash. They both came out of the store looking for him until they got a call from Tiffany. She had gone into a store with Ava and came out alone as well. The hunters probably went through the back or the employee area. When I checked those cameras, they had been disabled for a while.

The phone goes silent, and I think he's hung up on me, so I pull my phone away and see we're still on a call.

"Silas?" This fucker better not hang up on me. I'm not in the mood. I'll find him if I have to.

After a moment he finally asks, "When were they taken?"

"Just a few hours ago." I grab my notebook and pen from my computer in case he has something useful to tell me.

"Has she transitioned?" I drop my pen.

"How did you kn—"

"Did you notice anything out of the ordinary with her?" he interrupts. What the fuck does he know?

"Silas, I ain't tellin' you shit. If you know something that can help us find her and Ezra, you better start talking now." I know I'm threatening a member of the council, and it can have serious consequences, but when it comes to Silas, he operates through different standards. Although he's a council member, sometimes I believe he only has his own interest in mind. I guess they all do, but Silas is different.

"I'll check my resources," he says and hangs up, leaving me in the dark.

I throw my phone on my desk. I found absolutely nothing and, with no leads, I need to get this pent-up energy out of me, or I'll end up wreaking havoc in my own warehouse.

I keep spare gym clothes in one of my drawers. I open the cabinet, pull out my duffle, and get up to leave.

I'm grateful I don't run into anyone on my way to the gym. I get into the building, and everyone gives me a friendly wave or greeting, but everyone's in their own zone. I'm not worried about snapping if people come up to talk to me. I wouldn't be a good alpha if I snapped at my people for asking questions.

I get to the lockers, unzip my duffle, and grab my clothes. I change quickly and head straight for the punching bag. We have sturdier bags than the ones humans use because of our strength. The sand inside a normal bag would explode with just one of our hits.

I pick up my boxing gloves but then change my mind and put them back inside my bag. I'll just hit it with my bare hands.

My knuckles are bloodied as I hit the bag over and over, taking out all my aggression and the shame I feel for not being able to protect my family.

Two hours later, I've tamed the beast for a while.

I sit on the bench and rummage through my bag in

search of my phone, but I can't find it. Then I recall leaving it back at my warehouse.

I've got to remember that we don't need phones, we have our mind link back. *"How's Kat doing?"*

"Fuck, you scared me," Benji says, and I chuckle. It's a little daunting when you can hear someone other than you and your wolf in your head, can't believe this used to be the norm for us. Now it freaks us out when we hear each other in our head. It sucked when we lost our connection, but when cell phones became popular, it was a good replacement. I guess now we don't have to worry about leaving our phones behind anymore. *"She's been in and out of it, but she ate."*

"How are her eyes?" Seeing them more vibrant was a sure shock. I can't get it out of my head that I've actually seen those eyes before. I'll have to talk to the guys and see if it looks familiar to them too.

"Still glowing violet," Ash answers. I wonder if it's going to go away or if it'll linger now that she's unlocked the power within herself.

I take a shower in the bathroom gym, get dressed quickly, and go back to my warehouse.

My mind is clearer now, and I'm ready to dig into everything that's been going on. I go to my desk and sit down. I log onto the computer to start making connections. There's something here I haven't figured out yet, but I intend to.

Krissy was sleeping with Theo, and they both knew Dante, which means Theo has to be a supernatural—even if we don't know what kind.

When Theo came here, we never speculated about him being supernatural, probably because Krissy was helping him hide his scent and his power. Krissy was way too powerful. If there was anyone that could mask a scent, it would be Krissy.

And then it hits me.

"Oh shit!"

Their friendship wasn't a coincidence. Dante didn't know shit about Theo being a supernatural. He only thought Krissy was a witch, but Krissy never told on Theo. Was it because Krissy loved Theo, or did they have a pact? I do remember Krissy talking out loud about how he couldn't do this.

Was she talking about Theo? It has to be. It's the only thing that makes sense.

"Now the real question is, who the hell is Theo, and why would he hide being a supernatural? Does he know what Kat is? If he does, is that the reason he wants to have custody of the kids?"

"I'm going to call Theo," Kat says, slowly looking around the table. I think she thinks we're going to object, and I want to, but I also want to see what Theo is going to say. She searches her pockets for her phone.

"No, not yet." She whips her head around, ready to chew me out. "Tyler needs to set up the equipment to track his phone." She thinks about it for a moment and nods her head in agreement.

"Plus, your phone is in your room anyway," I add. That makes her stop looking.

"I need to get it to make sure no one calls about the kids." She stands back up.

"All your calls and messages have been forwarded to Tyler's phone," I say, and she sits back down. Ash can see everything on her phone anyway, but when I see him staring daggers at me to keep my mouth shut, I don't say what I'm thinking out loud.

"Oh, and I guess Ash can see everything I see anyway," Ash flinches. Serves him right for being a snoop.

"We need to get you checked out." Benji switches the conversation trying to diffuse any situation that would have arrived. He looks down on his phone, reading his message. "Doc and Amara are here." He stands up from the chair.

Finally, I need to know my mate will be okay.

"I'm fine." Kat sits back on her seat folding her arms like a stubborn child. "I don't need to be seen—I just need my kids back." Her leg bouncing up and down is the only indication that she's anything but *fine.*

"That's what we're working on, but first we need to make sure you aren't going to collapse on us again." Ash folds his arms too, mimicking her position. It does nothing but irritate her. The corner of her eye twitches like she wants a fight.

Ash won't budge on this. We have no idea what it means now that she used The Kiss of Death on herself, and her eyes haven't turned brown since.

"We have eyes on his office. We will get reports if Theo shows up or if the kids are spotted. Believe me, Kat, we're on it." I wanted to go with my guys, but I can't leave without knowing Kat will be okay. Tyler leaving was one thing. He didn't have to go far and it's still on our property. I have to drive three fucking hours. It's not happening until I truly know she's in good shape.

"What about the house?" Oh shit. I never told her.

"Everything is cleared out," I say, remembering the day I went there. There were no lingering smells to indicate that someone had been there recently.

"Wh . . . What do you mean everything was cleared out? My belongings?" Kat's full focus is on me, but her gaze doesn't scare me, it excites me.

"No, I mean the whole house is empty," I say, running my finger down my knife.

"I checked on it, and there's been no house listing. Theo still owns it," Benji adds.

"Huh?" She's looking at the table puzzled but says nothing else.

"I'm here!" Amara exclaims, Kat drags her eyes over to hers and a small smile appears on her face. She's followed by Dr. Jones.

They smile and nod at us while Amara blurts out, "Honestly, Kat, why didn't you call me?" Amara puts her hand on her hip. "I would've been there with you." She would have been encouraging too, and if something much worse would have happened, she would've done anything to keep my mate alive.

"No, you would've called us, right Amara, if she tried doing anything foolish," Ash scolds his long-time friend.

Amara simply ignores him. "Let's get you checked out. We'll go to the room where Benji and Tyler stayed before they were taken to the hospital."

Kat cringes like she's trying to forget when Benji and Tyler almost died. I am too. I still can't shake the feeling that I almost lost my brothers. I don't know what I would've done without them.

We get up from the dining table and make our way across the hall. Ash opens the room. "Sit," he tells Kat. She glares at him before she rests in one of the beds.

The smell of alcohol is strong in this room, and it's always sterile. It always messes with my nose and makes me want to sneeze, but I hold it in. I stand in the corner of the room. This is a better vantage point where I can see everyone without people realizing I'm here.

Benji sits behind her while Tyler stands next to the bed.

"I'm fine," she tells Doctor Jones. "They're just making a big deal out of nothing." Her violet eyes get brighter.

"She's fine. You guys are just making a big deal out of nothing," the doctor says, repeating exactly what she said. I look at his eyes, and they are glazed over. I look at Kat's and they're more vibrant than they were just a second ago.

"Shit!" Amara says as she leans against the wall and watches in awe, then quickly looks away with slight fear.

"Now we know the reason why her kind was hunted." Ash watches her intently. He's sitting on the chair on the opposite side of her. "I've seen her do it to Dante. There was so much going on that night, I just didn't process what really happened." He looks her dead in the eyes. He isn't afraid of her power. I look at my brothers and none of them are anxious.

I grab my knife from my pocket and twirl it around as I walk toward my mate. I don't want her to think I'm frightened. I want her to know that I support her. Well, not what she did to Doc exactly, but then again, she has no idea what she just did.

"She was only able to do it when her emotions were heightened and that was only because she turned into a wolf. The shifter magic was trying to let this magic out."

Amara's voice is in awe. She's still not looking directly at her friend but she can't help but be impressed.

I stand next to Ash and gently say, "Release the doc."

She turns her eyes over to me. "No."

She doesn't know she's doing it. "Az, leave me alone." I feel the pulse of her power, and I want to comply.

"She's like a vampire who lures victims but, instead of humans, she can lure supernaturals. And that's what makes her dangerous," Amara continues, her voice full of curiosity and excitement. "I bet this is the reason Krissy wanted Kat so badly. She knew about her power and wanted to take it like she did the power of our ancestors, like she did to you guys. With all the magic that was inside of her, this was the only one that she truly wanted. The control of other supernaturals. It's a dangerous power to have."

"Katarina, release the doc." She turns her eyes over to Ash.

"No." She crosses her arms.

"How are you resisting it?" Amara questions us.

"I feel the pull, and it tries to grab me, but it can't quite grasp me," I answer.

"Maybe it has to do with us being her mates." Benji grabs her waist and her body sags against his.

Benji whispers in her ear, "Let him go, Kitty Kat. He's only here to help you." That seems to pull her out of her trance.

"Oh God, I'm so sorry." She shakes her head in confusion and embarrassment.

"What happened?" Doctor Jones looks around the

room confused. He scratches his head trying to put the pieces together.

I open my mouth to speak, but Ash beats me to it. "You know how vampires can control humans?"

"Yeah, of course." He lifts his brow. He has no clue where we're taking this conversation.

"Katarina did the same to you." He takes a step back from my mate. He then looks at Kat again.

"H-How?" he finally asks.

"I should go." She gets up to leave, and her cheeks turn bright red in embarrassment as tears form in her eyes.

"Kat, we need to make sure you're fine," Amara says finally looking in her eyes.

"She's right," Doctor Jones pipes up. "I'm not upset, but I would rather you not use your powers on me again." He chuckles, but there's a hint of nervousness there.

"Yes of course," Kat replies, sitting back on the bed.

The way she constantly looks down, I know she's feeling extremely guilty. The doc checks her out, and she complies with everything he asks.

"Where the tattoo used to be still looks pretty raw," he says as he shines his light way too close for my liking. Throughout the whole checkup, I have had the urge to push him back a step or two to provide them with some distance. "This is going to take a while to heal up. It was infused with magic and then you used your weapon that's known to be deadly. I'm not sure if it'll heal completely or if it'll leave a scar." Her body slumps, she was probably expecting the worst and that's the reason she was trying to avoid the checkup.

"I have to go examine other patients at the hospital. Call me immediately if anything occurs," he says as he starts putting his equipment away in a suitcase.

She nods her head, "Thanks Doc."

Amara pushes herself from the wall with her leg that was propped up as Doc leaves us to seek other patients at the hospital.

She speaks to Kat gently. Probably afraid my mate might use her powers on her.

She uses her own magic to assess Kat's. Her assessment takes longer, so we sit around and wait patiently.

"Everything looks good on my end," Amara says, "but keep an eye on her." She looks at each of us. "With her heightened emotions, her magic might activate even when she doesn't realize it." She means like what happened to the doc. "Take this, Kat."

Kat takes the vial from her hands. "What is this?" She brings it up, inspecting it. The glass is clear and the contents are blue.

"It's to help you relax. Trust me, you need it." She tips the vial and pours the contents down her throat.

Once she's done, she gives it back to Amara. "Tasty." She licks her lips making sure she tastes every drop.

"How exactly will it make me *relax*?" Kat asks.

"It's a little something to help you sleep." Kat's eyes widen.

"Amara, I've already sle . . ." She doesn't finish before she slumps backward, but Benji is there to catch her.

I care about my mate's kids, and I want to protect them from whoever took them away. If it's Theo, I hope we finally get the chance to kill that man once and for all. But after what she experienced today, she needs rest.

The next day, I pace around my room. Ava and Ezra have been gone for a day now, and we haven't gotten anywhere. My guys tell me that no one has been in or out of Theo's office building.

I told them to go inside early this morning. It turns out, everything is still there. I don't know whether to be relieved or upset. I guess this means we'll just have to keep waiting for him to show up eventually.

I'm at Tyler's warehouse. My brothers and I stand off to the side with Tyler and an annoyed but nervous Kat. She's a little angry since Amara gave her the potion. She does look refreshed though. She needed her rest.

There are other supes in here doing God knows what on their computers. I don't even offer to help because the last time I did, I completely destroyed one of my brother's computers.

He hounded me until I bought him a new one. It cost me a pretty penny. Never doing that shit again.

So I continue to pace around, waiting for the opportunity to be able to leave here and go look for the person who took them.

"Go ahead and dial his number." Tyler signals to everyone in the room as he sits on the computer with our beta Matt.

Kat picks up her phone with shaking hands. Beads of sweat come down her brow.

It rings for a long time then goes straight to voicemail. I wonder if he's changed his number.

I want to punch something, anything, to get rid of this anger. It looks like Tyler already went to the gym this morning to get his aggression out.

"Try again," Tyler says from his station.

Kat dials the number and puts it on speaker again. I don't think he'll pick up, but after the fourth ring he answers. "Theo," my mate says in a small voice. I hate that she even has to say that man's name.

"Oh, Kat. Thank you for doing me a favor and killing Krissy." Kat's whole body freezes. That's not what we were expecting to hear. We're all stunned, but we should've already known. "I couldn't kill her myself because of a blood oath we made, and she was holding onto the power I needed. I had to promise her something that she wanted— your power," he confirms Amara's suspicions. "I didn't think you had the power in you, but after all these years, it was only dormant. I should have known. I was with you for a long time, but I just thought you were defective." There's a collective growl between us all. I can't wait to get rid of this worthless trash.

"I don't know what you're talking about," Kat says as Tyler signals her to keep the conversation flowing.

"Don't pretend you don't know. The bursts of powers started showing up when you got bit by that idiot." Wow, and here I thought they were close, but both of them never liked each other.

"Theo, do you have the kids?" her voice cracks, and I want to comfort her, but she needs to keep her head clear to deal with this man.

He chuckles, that's the only indication we need.

He has them.

"Listen Kat, as much as I want to chit chat, I know Tyler is tracking me, so we're going to have to cut this short. Just know that I'm coming for you." He hangs up before she can say anything else.

"Shit! Shit! Shit!" Tyler shouts, his frustration getting the best of him, and he grabs his screen and throws it on the floor along with the equipment that was attached to it. Everyone in the room stops what they're doing to stare at us. "I was so close, but he knew we were trying to track him." He puts his hands on the side of his face in defeat. If he had long hair, I could imagine him pulling his strands out.

"I'm sorry," I say, feeling like this is all my fault. I should've kept him talking for longer. I was pretty fucking nervous and absolutely shocked. I thought I was going to throw up my breakfast.

I still can't believe the words that came out of Theo's mouth. I mean, I know they're the truth. There's no point in lying, but was anything about our situation real? That leaves the question of whether Ava will have my powers or his. I should have asked him what he was. I hate how easily I was fooled by that man.

I only hope that when he realizes Ava can't shift, he won't try to hurt or kill her. But what if she has my powers? Will he sell her out to the council?

Before my mind wanders to the worst-case scenarios, Tyler comes to stand in front of me and holds onto my shoulders.

"No, don't apologize, Kat. It's not your fault. Theo knows a lot about us, more so than we know about him." There's a feeling deep down in the pit of my stomach that makes me anxious. There is more to this man than I ever knew. The thought that I actually lived with him scares me the most. He was hiding something in plain sight, and I never suspected any different. Ash did ask me about him being a supernatural, but I shrugged it off. There's no ignoring it now that he basically admitted to it.

I walk away from Tyler and go to pick up the mess on the floor. I need a distraction, there are too many rampant thoughts crossing my mind, and none of them are helpful. A few people come over to help us pick up. Once Tyler's calm enough, he grabs a broom to sweep up the shards of glass littering the floor.

"So the man knows a whole lot about us, but we know nothing about him," Az says as his face twists in anger. He doesn't like that at all and neither do I. He stands still in his position, not making a move to help us clean.

"Do we have anything else about his past that I can check out?" Az asks as he steps away from our group, choosing to stand alone in a corner instead. I think he hates that we currently have everyone's attention. If he could make himself disappear, I think he would.

"I've checked absolutely everything, chased every crumb. I've given you everything I found." He sighs walking back to his desk with his head hanging low like he's debating his next words. I don't like the look of defeat on his face, and I open my mouth, but before I can get a word out, he says, "I did find something else." He pulls a piece of paper from his pocket and unfolds it.

That stops Az from blending himself further into the shadows. "Smart Technology." Tyler says as if we should know what that means. We wait a moment before he begins again, "I found the location of the woman with violet eyes." He gazes at me then, and his eyes are full of sorrow. "She could have answers for you, Kat." My heart thunders in my chest. Is this it? Am I one step closer to finding out who I really am?

I don't want to get too excited just in case it's a dead end, but it's kind of hard not to be slightly thrilled at the idea that I may finally be getting the answers I've been searching for. After a hard day, I need some good news. I need to know that something is finally going our way. I need to keep the hope that everything will be fine.

"Oh, so that's where you were last night?" Ash questions, almost accusingly, as he rubs his chin in thought.

"I had to make sure that clue is legit and—I think it is." Tyler walks back to his chair and slumps down on it like revealing this information has tipped him over the edge in exhaustion.

"Where was my invite?" Benji narrows his eyes at Tyler.

"The more people that stayed with Kat the better. I

didn't want to take anyone else. But if you guys are really worried, I took Matt with me."

My eyes swing over to Matt, and he gives us a little wave and smile before he goes back to whatever he was doing on the computer.

"We should go check it out," I say eagerly. It'll give me something to do while Tyler can figure out where the hell my ex-husband is hiding my kids.

My wolf spits on the ground in anger at the thought of Theo holding them hostage.

"We should go find him now! We need to find our kids," she shouts in my head, baring her teeth, saliva dripping from her canines, and I know she's at her limit.

"I want that too, but you heard Tyler. He has no leads. He'll mess up though, and once he does, we will be ready," I reason, trying to calm her down.

My wolf gets antsy, and I know I have to let her out of her cage soon. She hasn't been able to run freely, but I'm scared that if I do, I won't switch back to being human until we've found our kids.

"And why is that a bad thing?" she asks in a harsh tone.

"Because you don't think before you act," I snap back.

"Again, why is that a bad thing?" She tilts her head in confusion.

It's no use fighting with her; she won't get it. So I ignore her for now, and she goes back to pacing restlessly.

Matt gets up from his seat. "This is the address of the place where it's rumored she's being kept. Our source was scared shitless of Tyler, so I have no doubt that he gave us the information he believes to be correct." He hands the paper to Ash as he inspects it.

"It's two hours from here," Tyler says, as he comes from behind me and grabs my waist. My body leans into his easily. "We'll find them, Kat," he murmurs into my ear. I just want it to happen now. I hate waiting, I hate Theo for kidnapping my kids, and I hate the fact that my power was hidden. My whole body vibrates in agreement.

I want to shut down and cry, but I have to be strong. There is no time to waste energy on crying. If I fall apart, I don't think I'll be able to get back up, and that's not what my kids need. They need a mom to stand up and fight.

"Az, can you send our people to this location and scope it out before we get there. We leave tonight unless we find a new lead on the kids." Ash gets into his role easily, directing people where to go.

Matt comes up to me. "Hey Lu—uh, Kat. Can I talk to you for a second?" I look around, but the guys are keeping busy.

I walk just outside of the warehouse, and Matt walks next to me. I wonder what he has to say to me that he didn't want any of my guys to hear. Is it serious? I look at his face briefly, and he looks like he's having a hard time putting what he wants to say into words.

If I'm going to be part of this community, I can't be afraid of what people bring up. "What's going on?" I ask him gently. I don't want to spook him, after all, this is the first time we've had a solo conversation.

"I-I uh, just wanted to apologize for hacking into your

phone. Ash made me do it, and well, he's my alpha. I really can't say no to him."

A bead of sweat trickles from his brow, he's nervous about what I'm going to say. "You're going to be our Lu—uh, leader, and I don't want you to think you can't trust me."

I smile, hopefully portraying the warmth and comfort I feel toward the betas. "I completely understand why you had to do it. I may not have liked the reasoning, but Ash was just watching over his pack, and he didn't trust me at the time. I've already forgotten about this."

"Are you sure?" he asks skeptically, looking down at the ground in submission, and it makes me feel sort of awkward.

I move to stand right in front of him, and when he looks up, I envelop him in a hug. "It's fine, Matt. I'm not upset and it's also fine to call me Luna. I know the guys are afraid to throw a lot at me at once, but I'm okay with the formal title, Kat is also okay." He hugs me back. We let go and he walks back inside.

Once we leave Tyler's warehouse, I message Theo to see if he responds. But it's been two hours and I get nothing. By now he probably already threw that number out.

"I'll find you, Theo," I promise out loud. I'll stop at nothing to find him.

CHAPTER 19

BENJI

In my storage facility, I'm putting together grenades for tonight. The three other guys and I are careful with them, making sure we don't drop them, or else that would be the end of us.

We don't have a concrete plan for the ambush. Ash is relying on Kat to use her powers and get them to do what she wants. It's actually a good idea, I just don't know if my mate will perform well under pressure or if she'll stall when the time comes. I hate that we put her in the center of it without proper planning, but I know she wants to help, and she won't be left behind.

If that idea tanks, it's a good thing we have our magic back. We can take out so many people with our power. If all else fails, my bombs surely won't. I pack the last one neatly in my case.

"I need you guys in my office," Ash tells us through our link.

"On my way," I reply as I grab my suitcase and head out the back door of my storage facility.

When I walk into the office, Tyler, Az, and Kat are all here along with Ash and our betas.

"This is your last chance to back out," Tyler tells Kat. They're both sitting next to each other opposite of Ash's desk. It looks like they've been having this conversation for a while based on the frustrated glances she throws his way.

"I'm going," she says with finality. Since the kids were kidnapped, I'm afraid to admit that I actually want her to be with us. But at the same time, we're going on a dangerous mission, and she may be safer here. It's a tough situation and my brothers see it too.

"Alright, everyone ready?" Ash asks. We all have on black tactical gear. It's easier to hide in the dark, plus it's comfy, and we can throw some punches if we need to. I glance at Tyler, and he looks like he can use a punching bag right about now.

We haven't done this in a long time. It brings back memories, both good and bad. We work so well as a team together, I'm curious to see if we still got it.

"Oh, we still got it," my wolf says.

We leave the house as a van pulls up. Joseph, another beta, is on the driver's side.

Kat's eyes trail the vehicle. "I've never seen this one before. Where do you keep it?"

"We've got a different location outside of our property where we store them. We use it for situations like this." Kat's eyebrows raise.

"Well that's probably a good idea. Don't want to lead

anybody to your property." She nods in understanding and clutches her backpack closer. I know she has her weapon in there. She carries it everywhere, which is good. I never want her to be without it.

"Damn right," I respond as I open the door and she steps inside. I go in after her, carrying the suitcase on my lap. I don't trust anyone but myself with this.

Az sits in the back passenger side while Ash and Tyler sit in the seat in front of us. When Ash closes the door, Joseph starts driving.

Kat looks behind us. "We have a group of guys following us." I don't tell her it's for her. She might fight us on this if she knew we brought them just to keep an eye on her. If anything on this mission goes wrong, they'll take her back to our place.

Everyone is silent the whole way there. Kat looks out the window. I can sense she's full of nerves, not only because we haven't found the location of where Theo is with the kids, but because she might potentially be getting some answers about who she is.

Two hours later Joseph says, "We're here."

We come to a complete stop. I'm kind of shocked when I look up at the tall building. It looks to have thirty stories. I actually was expecting something out in the middle of nowhere. This place is surrounded by many big businesses.

If there is something here, then whoever came up with this place is smart to hide it in plain sight.

It's late enough that some of the windows in the building are dark, and people have left work for the night.

There are two guards outside. It's the only building that has any visible security.

I find myself wanting to laugh. With our powers and Kat's, no one can hold us back.

We park a couple buildings down, and the rest of our team parks right behind us.

"Last chance to back out," I whisper to Kat. "We won't be upset. Actually, we'd be relieved." I smile innocently.

She narrows those deep violet eyes on me. "I'm going, and that's final." She scoots to the front to prove her point.

Ash looks behind me, and I shake my head. He sighs but there's nothing we can do. If she wants to go, that's her choice.

We climb out of the van, and as we get near the building, Tyler says, "Act like you're drunk and make as much commotion as you can."

We laugh loudly and stumble every few steps. "Hey, get out of here. This is private property," the security guard with the red hat says.

They're both supernaturals, vampires. I'm curious to see if it will work on them. I hand Ash the suitcase and grab Kat, pushing her against the glass. I hold onto both of her hands and pin them on top of her head before I hover over her, gently nipping at her bottom lip.

The other security guard nudges us. "Do your thing, baby." I let go of her arms, and she faces our first victim.

Her eyes get brighter before she opens her mouth and says, "Take a two-hour break." His eyes glaze over and he walks away.

"Oh shit, it worked," I shout, Ash hands me back the

case. "It works on vampires, too." I'm not going to lie, I had my doubts. Vampires are usually the ones able to compel humans to do whatever they want.

"Wh-what did you just do?" The other vamp with the hat stutters.

"I guess you aren't the only one that can make others do what you want." Kat smirks. The guy tries to run away, but Az holds onto his neck, steadying him before he gets a chance to leave.

"Your shift is over. Go home." He stares off into space before he starts walking away.

Kat jumps up and down with glee. "I did it. See, I told you guys I'm useful." She puts her hand on her hip.

"Aren't there cameras around here?" Kat asks, looking around the building.

"I disabled them all before we came here," Tyler responds as he tries to pull the door open. "It's locked, Az."

"On it," he says as he pulls out his tool kit from his chest pocket.

He gets on his knees, inserting the metal tools into the lock. It only takes him a minute to unlock it.

He pulls it open and we walk in. There's someone sitting at the front desk with headphones on, but she hasn't even noticed we're here.

Kat goes straight to her. She looks up and is startled by our presence. She looks at the door as worry edges the corner of her eyes.

"Who let you in?" she asks as she picks up the phone. Probably to call more security. Kat puts her hand on top of hers and the receptionist immediately pulls away.

"You're very exhausted, and you're going to take a five-hour nap." The girl nods her head as her eyelids fall heavy. She crosses her arms over the desk and lays her head on top. In less than a minute, she's knocked out and snoring.

"We need reinforcements," Ash says.

Tyler calls the rest of the guys. In two minutes, all fifteen guys are here.

"There are many more sections to this building that we're aware of. We need you guys to do a thorough sweep. We're going to have you check floors fifteen and up, and we'll check fourteen and below."

"Got it, alpha," they reply in unison. I grab the girl's badge and head to the elevators with the rest of them.

We push the top button and walk in. Tyler selects the fourteenth floor. "No one but your victims know we're here, Kat. The footage they're seeing is from a couple days ago. They think it's live."

Kat's eyes widen at that remark, but she doesn't get to say anything before the doors open back up.

"We'll stay together while the rest of your lovers check the floor."

"Shouldn't we be searching too?" Her eyes wander to their retreating backs. I put the suitcase down.

"We're keeping watch, making sure no one surprises us." I lean against the wall. To an outsider, I look relaxed, but on the inside, I'm on edge.

"Oh well, that makes sense." She stands on the other side of the elevator.

I figure we can do a little chit chatting to calm her nerves and mine too.

"So—" Her eyes go straight to mine, and I've gotten her full attention. "Remember that time I said there was one female to four males."

"Mhmm," she says as she watches the area to make sure nothing out of the ordinary will surprise us.

"Well I lied." She whips her head back toward me. "I had two moms and one dad." She scrunches her brows in confusion.

"Then why the hell did you tell me there were four to every female?" she whisper-shouts.

"I was so smitten by you, and I still am," I add with a smile to reassure her and hopefully get her drawn eyebrows to relax a bit. "Well . . . I was talking about us. When I said that I was thinking about you and us. I didn't want to scare you, but I also wanted you to be aware that you could be with all four of us if you wanted to."

She narrows her eyes. "There's no standard?"

"It varies with each pairing." I look around waiting for the guys to come and save me from the conversation I just put myself in.

"Anything else you need to *clarify*, Benji?" she asks.

I grin widely at her, and she rolls her eyes, knowing that I'm about to say something cheesy. "Just that you're the most perfect woman I've ever laid my eyes on." She scoffs, but her cheeks redden.

Thirty minutes later, they come back. "Place is clean. I can't get a read on whether or not this space is actually used." I get what Ash means. The place smells like chlorine, there's no telling if humans or supernaturals use this place.

We check the rest of the floors and come back with

nothing. Az is on the phone with our team. When he hangs up, he relays the information, although we've all already heard it.

"So it's the same on every level. They can't tell whether or not people actually work here or it's a hideout for something else."

"What a waste of time." Kat's voice cracks, and the hope in her eyes diminishes. We step into the elevator to head back down to the lobby.

Az takes one look at his mate and loses it. I hate seeing her like this too. "There has to be something we're missing. Something that doesn't show up on the plans we had."

He punches the steel right below all the buttons and the elevator stops. "What the hell?" Tyler questions.

A metal door swings open. We bend down on our knees to take a closer look.

"It looks like we need a badge," Ash says.

"We're in luck." I pull out the receptionist's badge I'd stolen.

"Hell yeah. Let's go figure this shit out." I scan the badge and the elevator resumes, bringing us down to a lower level. This was the difference between our plan and the one the receptionist had.

I look at my brothers and their bodies are tense, waiting for a fight. Right before the steel doors open, we push Kat to the back for safe keeping.

They slowly open to reveal a space that looks nothing like the other offices we've searched.

Jackpot!

"What is this place?" Kat whispers. Now I wish she

would have listened and stayed behind, but she's got a mind of her own, and we let her do what she wants because she's our mate, and we want to make her happy.

"I'm not sure," I respond. It looks like a facility of some sort. What the fuck is Smart Technology, and how have we never known about it?

We walk through the building with our ears on high alert. We move as a unit the way the council trained us. Fucking pieces of shit, all of them. I know for sure there's someone controlling them. They're supposed to have equal leadership, but that isn't the case. They fear whoever is in charge, and I have a feeling he's the one that made us do the dirty shit we didn't want to do. We were able to get out, but since Krissy admitted they were the ones who made her kill the witches to get her magic, it feels like they took away our powers so that we weren't a threat.

"Uh, guys . . ." The way Tyler's voice rises in worry has my skin prickling. "I think you should sit this one out, Az. Go to the car and wait for us there." Az stiffens next to me, but he walks past me anyway. Tyler tries to block him. "I don't think this is a good idea, man," Tyler pleads. "Sit this one out." Tyler enunciates each word clearly as if to make him understand that what's on the other side will cause Az harm.

Az punches him in the stomach, and it was totally unexpected. "Low blow, man," I say as Tyler doubles over in pain. I pat him in the back as Ash and I go through.

Kat stays behind to make sure Tyler is alright. She clearly hasn't ever seen us brawl before. We all like to spar with one another. It's a stress reliever. I'm sure she will lose her shit when she sees us really fighting in the ring.

I drag my eyes to all the monitors. There are one hundred kids from ages five to twenty-one. They have dark circles under their eyes and look really skinny.

Now I know what Tyler was trying to shield Az from. I drag my eyes to the man in question. He's still as a statue, clenching his jaw tightly as he looks around.

When Tyler recovers, he comes in with Kat. He has his phone in hand, probably calling Matt.

But what really paralyzes me is seeing the kids in cages. Tyler gets to one of the computers and types something in. I have no idea what the hell he's doing, but I think he's trying to figure out the location of the kids and how to get them out of there.

Kat gasps when she sees all the children on the screen, and her face pales. "Are my kids there?" Her eyes roam quickly through every screen.

"Uh, Tyler, who gave you this clue?" Az says, his piercing blue eyes staring at my brother.

He leans against the wall before answering. "It was Silas." I watch as Kat's eyes grow huge in surprise. "Not only that, but this is the place I tracked the camera to when Az and Kat went into the tattoo shop."

My brothers and I start shouting at once. "What the fuck, Tyler?"

"You know not to trust that man." We know never to trust him. He's the one that exploited our weaknesses to get us to work for the council.

"I know, I know, but he said that there might be something in here to help us find the lady with violet eyes, and I had to take the chance."

"Did you meet up with Silas last night?" Az questions. His jaw clenches tightly as he pulls out his knife and twirls it between his fingers.

"No, it was a guy who owed me a favor. I scared the shit out of him using our power, so I know he wasn't lying. He deals in secrets. I asked him if he knew of this place, and when he said yes, I asked him who owned it. He told me someone from the council, but he didn't know the person's name. I tripled checked by having my buddy Agent Cooper check into this and was given the same information. "

"No sign of our kids," Ash answers Kat as her eyes flick rapidly over each computer screen. She visibly deflates, but based on her posture, she's relieved that they're not being used for science experiments. I just hope they're not some-where much worse.

Kat watches Az carefully. She doesn't know much about his past. She stands right in front of him, but it's as if he isn't registering what's going on. She places one hand gently on each side of his face. "Az," she says in a soothing tone. "Look at me." He drags his eyes back to her. "Let's get out of here."

"Hey! You aren't supposed to be in here." A guard appears in the doorway and points his pistol right at Kat.

I panic, and in one swift movement, I open my case, grab a grenade, release the pull pin and lever, and I throw it in his direction. My brothers don't hesitate to move out of reach. The guy looks down at it, not really registering what it is, and when he does, he backs away, touching his head piece to communicate with someone. As he runs away, he tries to squeeze the trigger of his gun when the bomb goes off and body parts start flying. It was a small one, but it still shook the floor.

The ringing sound of the alarms going off is sensitive to my ears.

We've been found. "We need to get out of here, now!"

CHAPTER 20

Az

The alarms are blazing throughout the facility. A clear indication that whoever owns this place knows we're here.

There is no way I'm leaving without knowing the location of those kids. I don't care if they're onto us. I'm not abandoning them to be science experiments. They look malnourished and who knows what else they've been through.

When I find the person who is doing this to them, I'm going to kill them.

"Tyler, call Matt and tell him to bring more vehicles." We didn't bring enough cars for them all. I don't give a fuck if they have to steal them. Our guys are resourceful, they'll find a way to get what we need.

"Already on it, brother. They're on their way." He knows me too well. He knew there was no way I'd be able to leave those children behind. Even if he didn't have the same childhood, I know my brothers would never leave these kids behind.

Memories of my brutal childhood flash through my mind, and I push them back. I can deal with those thoughts later, just not right now. I need to focus on what's in front of me. A group of five guards appear right in front of us with guns pointed straight at our heads.

We didn't want to do this, we didn't want to use our power on them, but we have no choice now. It's either us or them, and it's not going to be us.

"They deserve to die. They watched as kids were experimented on. We should make them pay and kill them all."

"Ready," Ash says, disrupting my wolf's thoughts.

"Ready," we say in unison. Less than a full second later, they're screaming, holding on to their heads. Blood pours from their eyes as they roll back and fall to the floor.

"What the hell?" Kat shouts. "That's your magic?" Oh no, we've scared her. I panic thinking she'll leave us. I've just found her, and I can't let her go. My hand trembles, and I grip my knife tightly. "That's so freaking awesome." She beams with admiration, and my body sags in relief.

"You're one of them," another guard says in disgust. He comes around the corner with a gun pointed at Kat. I'm not sure why he'd say that, maybe because we killed his friends. "You'll be locked up and experimented on."

Just as we suspected, this place is used to poke and probe those kids. I'm going to kill the person slowly, peeling off their flesh. I can already hear those sweet screams in my ear.

Does Silas know? If he does, then he deserves to be punished.

Everyone involved with this place deserves nothing less than a slow, painful death. The guard laughs like a maniac. "You'll be killed by his hand."

"Yeah, not happening," I say as I throw the knife and hit him between his eyes.

"We gotta keep moving," Ash says as he steps over the bloodied body. I retrieve my weapon, but not before wiping the blood on his clothes.

We check through the rooms lined up on each side of the wall, but they're all closed. Those monitors have to lead somewhere, but my biggest fear is that the kids are locked up in an entirely different building.

Benji sets off a bomb in front of the locked doors, and it explodes within seconds, denting the steel. He sets off another one, and this time it breaks the door down. We immediately walk in and discover ten teenagers huddled together. I let out a long sigh in relief. They look to be between the ages of thirteen to eighteen, and the fear in their eyes enrages me. Who would do such a thing to these kids? Oh yeah, sick bastards. I should already know the world is full of them. No matter if you're supernatural or human, every species has them.

"Come on, you're okay," Benji speaks softly, trying not to spook them, but they still look frightened. I would open my mouth and say something, but I usually make people uncomfortable. I wish I knew the right words to help these kids with easing their anxiety.

"You look familiar," the youngest boy in the group,

says quietly, looking at Benji. He looks to be around thirteen. My brother walks up to the scared boy, and he flinches away from my brother. The other kids move toward the boy as if to protect him. I don't know how they think they can take Benji down, but I like that they stick together. It makes me wish I had someone that stood up for me in my early years. That's why I value the tight bond my brothers and I have now.

Benji crouches down to the boy's level and raises his hand, resting it on his shoulder.

"I can assure you, I've never been here before, and if I had, I would have rescued you a lot sooner," my brother answers with deep regret like this is his fault, but none of us could have known. He drops his hand and steps back toward us.

"I'm going to go up and get the guys to come down here and start taking the kids to the vehicles." Tyler looks over to Benji. "Give me the card." Benji tosses it to him.

"Be careful," I tell him. He nods and heads out the way we came in, stepping over the broken pieces of the door and wall. We walk deeper into the facility. There are operating rooms and lots of jars with random shit in them.

"Benji and Kat, stay with the kids." They're the only people I trust with the kids. I know if I was in their position, I would be skeptical about new faces offering a way out. I've been screwed before, and these kids probably have been too. We can't blame them for being scared of leaving here with us. I just hope my brother and my mate can help them see their options. "Ash and I will keep opening more doors." Benji hands me the suitcase. It's enough for three more doors. I'm counting five in total that might have kids.

Ash and I set three bombs in front of each metal door, and like the first one, the doors crumble. As we peek inside, more kids huddle in a corner, maybe ten per room.

"We need to open two more doors," Ash says, but we've used all the bombs.

"It's going to take me a while to break into these locks." I look at the blaring red lights on the alarm system. "And that's time we don't have."

"What do you have in mind?" Ash asks. He already knows I have a plan in my head.

I look around but find nothing that can be useful. "I'll go check the security guards to see if any of them have keys."

I sprint down the hallway to where Kat and Benji are. I see our betas starting to take more of the kids. I go down another hallway where we killed those monsters.

I check through the first three guards and come up empty. Two left. I check the one I knifed through the forehead.

Bingo!

This fucker has keys. I just hope they work. I sprint down the hall and take another right. Everyone watches me and sensing my urgency, they move to the side to let me through.

I dangle the keys in front of Ash. "I hope one of these works." I go to one of the doors and try several keys before finding the one that unlocks the door. These look to be older kids between eighteen and twenty-one. They have the same fear in their eyes, but also a fire the younger kids didn't have. They look like they are willing to fight if they have to.

"Who the fuck are you?" a girl with short blue hair voices. She's a shifter, actually— They're all wolves like us.

"Hey, Ash, have you noticed that it's only shifters in here—specifically wolves?" I look at each of them as if they hold the answer on why only wolves are being locked up.

"Yeah, I've noticed that too," he answers with a puzzled expression.

"Why are you guys here?" A brave girl begins to speak. I look down at her hands, and she clenches and unclenches her fist.

"How many of you guys are here?" I ask, wanting to make sure we get every single one of them out of here.

"You answer my question first." The girl folds her hands trying to look tough, but I can smell her fear.

"We were looking for—something, but instead we found you guys." I decided to give in and give her an answer.

"What were you looking for?" she pries for more.

"I answered your question and now you answer one of mine. Why are you guys locked up, and how did you get here?"

"That's two questions, but I'll answer the first one. We are shifters, and we all have magic. We were told that only a sliver of the shifter population has magic." Umm . . . what? I look back at Ash and he looks just as confused.

"How did you end up here?" Probably a dumb question, but I need to ask if only to confirm that they were taken.

"Nope my turn," she says, and I try not to growl in annoyance.

"Where are you planning on taking us, and are we experiments?" Fair question, and I'm actually glad they're skeptical about this situation.

"With our pack," Ash replies, looking at each of them as they cower. It's the alpha energy.

"We're planning on finding your family, and to answer your next question, no, we won't experiment on any of you," Ash continues.

They all laugh and we look at each other before looking at the group in front of us. "Our families are all dead."

Chapter 21

Ash

"All your families are dead?" I ask, I must have misheard them. I step closer and immediately remember that I don't want to spook them, so I take a step back. I don't want them to feel like we're a threat.

Our auras already give out alpha energy. When we walk by, supernaturals and humans can sense our energy. That's why people don't usually fuck with us. The ones who do, well, if they're stupid enough to try, the only thing they remember is our faces before they black out on the floor. I don't want to scare the kids more than they already are.

They've been through shit. You can tell by the way their bodies sag with exhaustion. They are malnourished and sickly from all the poking and probing that was done to them.

"Our parents are dead," Another guy answers slower this time. "By hunters." Az and I growl in response. I'm glad Benji isn't here to hear this, or else he'd lose his shit. He's very testy when it comes to hearing about hunters, especially in reference to killing family members.

"I thought we got rid of all hunters?" I turn to Az. "What the fuck is going on? They just started showing up out of nowhere." He shrugs, just as confused as I am. I'm glad we both saw them with our own eyes because we wouldn't have believed these kids otherwise. We made sure we got rid of every single one of them. We did it all for Benji.

"They work for him." A blonde kid with blue eyes steps forward.

"Who is *him*?" I ask curiously. Maybe they can give us more information on the person that owns Smart Technology.

"A shifter that works with the hunters seems out of the ordinary; it just doesn't click," Az replies. "They're very nature is to hunt us."

The brunette shrugs. "Maybe they had a deal."

"I guess everything we thought we knew is absolutely false. Here we thought that the almighty council wanted to protect the best interest of the supernaturals, but now we know how wrong we've been." Az looks like he's about to burst with rage. I need to get these kids out before he freaks them out and they won't want to leave with us.

Katarina and Benji come into the room, and my attention is on my mate when there's a collective gasp. I turn around to see what has them so surprised. They're staring at Katarina, and I don't like the way their eyes widen.

"The guys have taken all the other kids out of here. Is this the last door?" Benji asks, looking back and forth between the kids and Katarina.

"What's going on?" he asks mentally.

"No clue, but they see something in Katarina," I answer. *"I've got it handled. Go get the others before we run out of time."*

Out loud I say, "There's two more. But you'll have to figure out what keys go in the lock." I hand it to Katarina and they sprint out of the room.

In the distance, I hear her ask Benji, "How are you guys talking? Why couldn't I hear it?" I don't focus on his response, instead, I bring my attention back here.

"She—" The girl with blue hair stutters. "She has violet eyes." How the hell does this girl have blue hair? It's been bugging me since I laid eyes on her. But there's no time to ask.

"Indeed she does. Does anyone else around here have the same color eyes?" I ask hopeful that we'll maybe be able to get answers for Katarina after all. This is the one thing I truly hope I can give her. Finding out who she really is.

"Yeah, but she's locked up tightly." Her eyes are full of sadness, and I know that when we find the woman, she won't be in good condition. I debate whether I want Katarina to go through with it. Maybe she's better off not seeing it. Maybe I should take a look before she does. "We have only seen her a handful of times."

"Where is she?"

"You go down this corridor and take two lefts. The door is sealed more so than ours was." So it means she's been kept hidden. She's a powerful tool if she can make supernaturals do what she wants them to do, and in the council's hand, that's absolutely dangerous. I wonder how long she's been held down here.

"We're ready to take the ones in here," Jacob says. All sets of eyes shoot to my beta, assessing him and wondering if they should trust him. I hate that look in their eyes. They're too young to have so much distrust in a person. I hate that they've been through so much without anyone helping them.

"It's your choice whether you want to stay or go," Az says, surprising me. I thought he'd try to take them all. "You already know what life is in here, why not give it a shot in the outside world?" He's giving them a choice. They probably have never had one before.

"For most of us, this is all we know," she says sadly, and my heart aches for them. The kids nod their heads in agreement. I can't imagine what this is doing to Az right now.

"All we can do is offer you guys a better chance at living," he says softly. I've never heard him speak so tenderly to anyone, not even Katarina. This situation is getting to him.

"Are you okay, Az?" I ask through our mental link.

He looks tense as fuck the way he grips the hilt of his knife, and he sighs deeply before answering, *"I don't know."*

The kids look at each other before answering, "We'll go." Az's shoulders sag in relief. He was going to have them make their own choice. That is the first step to what freedom will be like for them. They'll finally have options.

"We have to go now!" One of our guards yells. "There are vans heading in this direction."

"How much time do we have?" Az asks, looking behind the entrance to the room.

"About fifteen minutes." Another one responds.

"You three," I point to the guys that just came down here. "Help us get the other kids. The rest of you start making your way to the vans."

Everyone moves at a quicker pace than they did before. We meet Benji and Katarina.

I grab Katarina's arm before she walks any further. She stops to look at me with an eyebrow raised, probably wondering why I've just stopped her from helping the other children.

"What's going on, Ash?" I let go of her elbow.

"The kids told me there's a person with violet eyes just like yours." I almost feel like her own eyes get brighter. Now that she cut the heart from her face, her eyes seem to glow.

"Where is she?" Katarina demands, taking a step closer to me. I want to grab her and comfort her, but this is not the time. We have a very limited window. We need to get what we came here for and go. Plus, we now have to transport one hundred kids out of here.

"I just want you to know . . ." I hope she doesn't go in there expecting a healthy woman. "The kids sounded sad for the lady, so I don't think she's in good shape." I'm scared of what we may find. I have to wonder if this is the reason the council wanted to make sure Katarina wasn't a *threat* to them or if it was because they wanted to use her as an experiment.

"I don't care, Ash. I need to find her." Her eyes glow brighter as her power leaks through. Once she notices, she shakes her head, probably trying to clear her mind.

"Are you sure you're ready, Katarina?"

She bites her lip before answering with determination. "I'm ready." It's why we came here originally, but I'm glad we found the kids along the way.

"Go," Az tells me through our mind link. *"We'll meet you guys there."* I look back to see my brothers rushing to get the kids out of their cells. Because that's exactly what this place is, a prison for them.

With that, we make a run in the direction the kids told us.

We come to an isolated room, and I try the knob, but it's locked. Kat pulls out the keys and tries to unlock the door, but there's no place to insert it.

"I don't think any of those are going to work," Tyler shouts, and I see all three of them sprinting toward us. He points at the scanner located off to the side.

Katarina and I both look at each other, surprised we missed the obvious handprint scanner.

"We'll just have to bring the dead body of one of the guards. Did anyone see which guard had keys?" Tyler asks. "That might be the one in charge."

"The one with the knife in between his eyes." With that, Tyler runs back, leaving us alone.

A minute later, he's hauling the dead man on his

shoulder like he weighs nothing. Tyler grabs the dead guard's hand and presses it against the red sensors. When the circles turn from red to green and the door unlocks, he throws the man on the floor with a loud thump.

When the door clicks open, we all look at Katarina. "I'll go first," Benji shouts over the alarm.

We're startled by a loud voice down the hall. "Alpha's, they're coming in hot. They'll be here in five minutes or less."

"Thanks Jacob," I tell him as he approaches us.

"All the kids are in vehicles. The guys will be here soon." By the guys, he means the rest of the betas.

"Wait for us up there." He watches me skeptically. "We'll be right behind you."

"Uhh . . ." He scratches his head. "We don't want to leave you guys here."

"That's an order." I hate doing this, but I really want them up there with the kids and helping keep an eye out. We've got our magic, now we can protect ourselves and Katarina.

With that, he runs away. We switch our attention back to the door. Benji pushes it open and stalls.

"Benji, what the fuck?" Az growls right behind him.

"Benji, get the fuck out of the way if you're not going to move," Tyler growls behind Az.

Katarina is right in front of me, and I take the rear. She looks behind me, but I only shrug. I have no clue what's going on.

"Hey, Benji?" No response. "You—okay?"

He finally moves and we make it past the door. I look at Benji.

This is not what we were expecting. I don't look around the room because the look of horror on my brother's face stops me from moving forward.

"Benji, are you alright?" Katarina asks as she walks toward him. His face pales, and he's too stunned to formulate words.

"Maybe you should go back to the van, Benji. You aren't looking too good," Az voices with his knife in one hand. He's as worried as the rest of them.

"Hey big brother," A feminine voice startles all of us. That stops Katarina in her tracks, and we finally turn around to see who spoke.

There is a girl standing on the other side of the huge room. She's the mirror image of Benji. Can this be his dead sister?

No, it can't be.

He's told us about his sister and how he lost her during a hunter raid. He went to a shop to go pick up her dress, and that's when they decided to attack. She was dating a boy whose father was a hunter.

"Are . . . are you working with the hunters?" Benji finally speaks up. He's holding so much tension in his jaw.

"Benji, it's not like that," she answers softly. I'm not sure what to think of her. If she wasn't his sister, we would've killed her without hesitation. Maybe it was for the best that we didn't see her first. I have no doubt Az would've thrown his knife or Tyler would have attacked without giving it a second thought.

My mind doesn't want to trail down that rabbit hole, but I have to wonder, and I'm sure my brothers are thinking this too. Did she help hurt those kids?

"Then how is it, Zoe? I've cried for you and made myself sick thinking I failed you." Yeah, and we extinguished the hunter population because of it, or at least we believed we did until recently.

Zoe? Oh fuck this can't be good.

The only time I've heard that name is the only time he told us about his baby sister. Could she be one and the same?

"It has to be. There is no other Zoe he's ever talked about," my wolf says slowly, our eyes drifting from our brother to his apparent sister.

Benji takes hesitant steps toward his sister and stops right in front of her. He takes notice like we all do that she isn't bound by any shackles or restraints. She looks like she's free to go anytime she wants.

She notices the same thing because she says, "I'm still a prisoner, Benji. I just—I just don't have shackles." She raises her hands toward us, proving that she's not held by anything physically.

Benji opens his mouth to speak, but he gets choked up. "I grieved for you, for our father and our moms, and this whole time you've been alive?" His voice is raw and full of anguish. His eyes are teary, and my heart goes out to my brother. It's a hard moment to witness.

Kat walks forward and stands next to him, grabbing his hand. He takes it in his and grips it like she's his lifeline, and maybe she is. I want to ask him if he's okay through our mind link, but I don't want to distract him from this moment.

"What are you doing here, Zoe?" Zoe's eyes finally roam to Kat's, and her eyes widen. Another emotion overtakes her body . . . fear.

"Benji, get away from her!" she screams in horror. She walks toward her brother and my mate. I don't like that at all. I don't know anything about this woman other than her being Benji's baby sister and someone who was supposed to be dead.

Az takes the closest side next to Benji, and I take over the other side. I don't want to hurt Zoe, but if she does anything to threaten my mate's life, I'll do anything to protect Kat.

Ignoring us, she stands in front of her brother, keeping a small distance between them. Zoe pays us no mind, and her eyes are still on Kat. The way her mouth twists in distaste at her presence makes me want to eliminate the threat. My hand begins to shake with adrenaline. We don't have much time, and I want Kat to get her answers, but Zoe is in the way.

"Benji," Ash warns him subtly, letting him know that he needs to make a decision now.

"I don't who the fuck you are, but I'm not letting you mess with my brother." In one swift movement, Zoe grabs the medical scissors from the table and goes straight for Kat.

Az immediately grabs Zoe's hand before it makes contact with our mate. "Benji!" he shouts. "Tell your sister to calm the fuck down or else I'll have to knock her out."

"Zoe, this is my mate." He pushes Kat behind him to protect her. Kat is short, and Benji towers over her, hiding our mate from Zoe's view.

"No." She shakes her head. The look of horror on her face makes me glad Kat can't see any of this. "It can't be."

She runs to another door. I didn't even notice it there. This is bad, I'm being too careless with our surroundings. Seeing Benji in shock and then finding out his sister is alive has made me forget about checking the area. I take a moment to really look at where we are.

There's equipment you'd see at a doctor's office. There are ten beds in total. I can imagine this is where they pick and probe those poor kids. I truly hope Zoe isn't one of the bad guys. I don't know what that'll do to Benji, but I can't let her live knowing she's hurt innocent shifters.

"What do you mean?" Benji asks, biting his lip and looking at his sister with confusion.

"I mean," she emphasizes, "that this is your mate." She runs to the back and opens a sliding door, revealing a woman in a large water tank, wearing a two-piece bathing suit.

"Is it the woman with violet eyes?" my wolf asks, our attention on what's in front of us.

"I think we finally found her." I sag in relief.

The woman looks oddly familiar, but—I can't pinpoint exactly why that is.

"Does she look familiar to anyone else?" Benji asks softly, echoing my thoughts.

"Probably because she's your mate," Zoe snaps, and Kat softly growls. Ash rubs her shoulders to reassure her that she's ours.

We walk further into the room. Zoe keeps her eyes on Kat. I get that this is Benji's sister, but he hasn't seen her in over a century; she may not be the person he remembers.

I stand next to Kat while Az takes the other side, and Ash doesn't move from the rear. Benji walks up to the tank.

"This is the woman we're looking for," Benji says as he gazes at the woman. I look around the tank trying to figure out how the hell we're going to take her out of here.

"Because she's your mate." Her sister rolls her eyes as if she doesn't understand why we don't believe her.

"No, no. It's like I've seen her before." Benji puts a hand on the glass.

"Benji, she's your mate. She was locked in here because of the prophecy."

"What prophecy?" Az asks, turning his head to the side, looking nothing like a human anymore. His animal side has taken over, and we have to make sure he doesn't pounce on Zoe. I know Benji would never forgive him if he hurt his sister.

We're stuck.

We need to leave this place before we get caught, but

now we have a giant tank and Benji's sister to figure out. How the hell are we going to get the woman out of the tank?

Her eyes are closed like she's in deep slumber. She has a mask over her nose and mouth to help her breathe in the water.

"The prophecy he's trying to prevent. The one where he'll be stopped." Still doesn't ring anything, but there's no time to ask her to explain.

Ash grabs Kat from behind, pulling her close to his chest. "This is our mate. I don't know who that lady in there is. She does look—oddly familiar, but I know without a doubt that she's nothing to us."

"Well that would suck for this poor lady," Zoe says, watching her.

"Why is she in here?" Kat speaks for the first time, and I hate it because Zoe's evil stare goes back on my mate.

She walks to the side of the tank and hits a red button, and the water starts to drain. "I can't let her out or else she'll die. She's been drained too much. This is the only way she survives. The water has magical properties that sustain her life force. She's tried to kill herself a couple of times but hasn't succeeded."

"Krissy tried to drain her of her powers, but I don't think it worked," Kat says softly. She's probably thinking about how it could've been her next if she had shown any signs of magic. Right now, I'm grateful Jess was able to hide her powers.

As soon as the water is gone, she opens her eyelids, and the first thing we notice are her eyes. They look exactly like

Kat's. Kat walks toward the tank, and Ash lets her go, but he keeps a close eye on Zoe as he walks closely behind her.

The way she stares at us gives me goosebumps. It's as if she recognizes us.

Kat puts her palm against the glass and the lady stares at it for a moment before she puts hers on there, mimicking Kat's.

"Can she talk?" Kat whispers, and Zoe narrows her eyes. I don't like the way she's looking at her. If she wasn't Benji's sister, I'd have gotten rid of her by now.

"Zoe, answer her," Benji snaps. Her eyes widen before they turn into slits.

"She can. But—she's very weak," Zoe says with a look of sorrow. If she feels this way about this woman, maybe she was able to care for the kids that were tested on.

"Are you related to me?" Kat asks.

She takes off her mask. "I don't know." The voice is low and weak.

"There were only a handful of us left before my capture." She turns her eyes to us like we're the cause of her pain, the reason she was locked up.

"I lived a beautiful life with my kid and my husbands. All it took was one day for my world to be destroyed." Her beautiful face morphs into anger.

"What are we?" Kat asks.

"We were called violet voyagers, feared by many supernaturals, and we've been killed off for our power."

"The person that held you hostage, what did he do to you?" Kat demands.

She laughs like a woman that has lost her mind. Kat

startles and takes a step back. Ash is there to rub her shoulders.

"He thought those four were my mates, and he was afraid of the prophecy, and it ended up happening anyway. I wish I could see his face before I die," she states.

Kat asks the question we're all thinking, "What is the prophecy?"

I want to ask why we should care about the prophecy, but I stay silent to let Kat get her answers.

"Chaos will happen on earth if he brings them back." Bring who back? I have so many questions. I look toward my brothers wearing the same expression on their faces. They want to know more but are keeping their lips tightly shut. "You're the chosen one, not all of us have that power."

"Why are you trapped in here?" I wonder if Kat sees herself in this woman. I wonder if she's afraid to be trapped like she is. I won't ever let her be trapped.

"Because for a certain time, I was useful to him, until he found out I didn't have what he was looking for," she responds as she looks at Zoe then back up at Kat. "He drains me of my power, the same as the kids in here."

"But why—why does he do it?"

"The man is frightening," she continues. "He's the supernatural our community should be afraid of, not us." Kat nods her head in agreement.

"He's the only one of his kind. He used me to control everyone around him. He used my family, and then he locked me in here to keep me from being able to sway him my way."

"What is he trying to do?" I ask.

"Open a portal that's been closed for a very, very long time."

"What's on the other side?" Kat asks.

"Danger," she responds, and I can feel a chill run down my spine at that one word.

"Guys we have to go. They're approaching," Az says as he looks down at his phone.

"Is everyone in the vans?" I ask.

"Yeah, everyone but you guys," Matt answers from the doorway.

"Leave me the keys to ours and go," Az tells him.

"But . . ." Matt's eyes widen, wanting to argue when he knows he shouldn't even try.

"I said go," Az shouts harsher this time. Matt hands me the keys and leaves.

"What's our power?" Kat asks quickly.

"We can sway supernaturals. We controlled kingdoms before humans took over. There's . . ." It sounds like she wants to say something else but stops herself. I don't think Kat notices.

Kat is speechless, but her violet eyes burn brighter than ever before.

Then the lady in the tank whispers, "Remember."

It crashes through us like a freight train, and we fall to the floor, holding our heads like our brains are about to explode.

"It's been Theo all along," Ash growls.

"This is his facility and he controls the council," I pant. Dread fills every fiber in my body.

"Now, Zoe," she commands. Zoe gets right to it, turning around facing the computer closest to the tank. Zoe starts typing furiously as the lady puts her mask back on. I don't notice the liquid dripping out of the tube of the mask until she closes her eyes.

The violet eyed woman is dead.

Chapter 23

Benji

It was Theo all along. He is the one behind all this fucking mess.

What makes me angry is that he was right under our fucking nose this whole time. He was in our home; we let him into our sanctuary. My claws come out from my fingertips ready to rip everything in sight.

My biggest regret right now is not killing him then and there. I don't have to look at my brothers to know they're thinking the same thing. If we knew she was our mate back then, things would have gone very differently, but that leaves the question, would we have made it out alive if we tried to attack?

Theo seems to be a very dangerous and powerful man. Recruiting Krissy made him untouchable. Now it all makes sense why he married Kat. But how did he know about my mate? How did he know anything? When you've been alive a long time, you can know where to look and who to track, but this was never on our radar. We were at a disadvantage.

I hate that we had our chance twice to kill him, and we missed the opportunity both times. I'm not letting him go next time.

I look over at my mate, and Kat looks like she's about to puke. Ash is keeping her steady, grabbing her shoulders while she sways back and forth. Az looks like he wants to destroy the whole room and look for someone to bleed out. It will suck for whoever decides to cross his path next.

I look over at Tyler, and he watches me with concern. I don't like it. It makes me feel like he thinks I'm one second away from breaking apart. I want to tell him I'll be fine, but the truth is, I don't fucking know if I'll ever be okay.

My wolf wants to get out of my human body and be near our sister. As soon as he saw her, he immediately recognized her. He wanted to shift as soon as he smelled her familiar floral scent that reminds us of the time we lived with the circus. That was back when everything was good and my parents were alive, before I became ruthless. Because underneath my playful exterior, I'm just as bad as my brothers.

I've lived my life thinking that because of me, Zoe didn't survive, because I was a drunken mess, I was more worried about sleeping around with different women in each town. The guilt ate me up every day. After the attack, it was unbearable. I thought about taking my own life a few times because I couldn't face my demons, and now Zoe is standing here in the flesh, healthy as can be.

She looks older now, her hair is longer, and she's taller. She looks more sure of herself, and she even carries herself with more confidence, but she'll always be my little sister.

Tyler is the only person other than me that has a sibling. The way he takes a long breath with so many deep emotions running across his face, I think he's putting himself in my shoes. What would he have done if *his* brother had died only to realize he was very much alive?

Tyler has calmed over the years, but when I first met him, he was completely different. I honestly thought he'd lose his cool and tear the whole place down in anger. I've always been calmer than any of the other guys, but right now, burning this place to the ground seems like a great idea.

I'm really trying not to lose my shit here. It's not the best place to do it in the middle of us taking those kids and having Kat with us. We need to get out of here, but my body can't seem to move. It's frozen in its spot. The others look to be in the same situation. I turn again to watch my sister, who was supposed to be dead long ago. I wonder what she'd think if she knew I killed her fiancé. He was a terrible person, but does she know that?

Loud noises assault my ears. I turn to look at the open door, I can faintly hear people yelling.

They've arrived.

I think they're sorting through the rooms right now looking for the kids.

The gunshots are banging through the walls, and I hope that everyone, including our betas, got out of the building. The noise is getting closer.

We sprint out of the room. I look behind me, and my sister is standing in front of the computer, smiling sadly at me. No, not again. I can't go through this again.

"We won't go through this again. We're smarter and faster and we know how to fight. We've had years of training," My wolf reminds me.

I don't know if she feels awkward coming with us, but there is no way I'm leaving her here for Theo. I now know what that man is capable of, and I don't want my sister in his path any longer.

"Let's go, Zoe!" I shout back near the entrance.

"I can't," she says with a sad smile as tears begin to well up in her eyes.

I take a step closer to her. "What do you mean you *can't?*"

"I mean, big brother, that I'm physically bonded to this place." My mouth hangs open, this was not what I was expecting. "Why don't you think I wasn't able to contact you?" This had crossed my mind earlier, but I didn't want to dwell on it too much, not until I had the chance to have an actual conversation with her, just the two of us.

She grabs my hand, and I have to try and find it in me to hold myself together when all I want to do is break apart. Her hands are so much bigger than I remember, but they're still so soft and warm.

"I had to, Benji, it was the only way to keep you safe. Theo knew where you were and knew everything about you. We made a pact. I helped keep people from discovering who he was, and in exchange, he wouldn't touch you." No, no, this can't be, I just found my sister. There's no way I can leave her behind after knowing she's alive.

I have no words, nothing comes out of my mouth. I

hear people outside of the door screaming, and I know my brothers are painting the halls red with our enemies' blood.

"I thought once Krissy died, I would be able to leave, but to my surprise, she wasn't the one who bound me here." I don't have time to question her because she's pushing me out the door.

"I need to protect you, Zoe." I have to. I wasn't able to on the day of the massacre. How can I leave her behind again?

"I've got it covered, Benji," she says, pushing me further away. "How do you think I was able to survive this long?" I stop walking and look outside at the bloodbath. My brothers have it handled. They don't try to rush me or scream at me to get going. They know I need time with my sister, and I'll forever be grateful to them for giving me this time.

"You're not the only sibling with magic." With one last push, she closes the door, keeping me on the outside, and I'm left wondering what the hell her power is.

I turn around slowly. My mind is processing the information that my sister is still alive. The next thing I know, I'm standing in front of the elevators. I look down to see Tyler's hand on my sleeve. I think he dragged me here.

I look at his moving mouth and shake my head, realizing he's talking out loud and speaking to me. I just wasn't processing anything.

"Wh-What did you say, Tyler?"

Without answering me, he grabs my shoulder and shoves me to the elevator. I look around noticing it's just him and me in here.

Where the hell are the others?

Chapter 24

Kat

I'm startled awake by the alarm on my phone. I grab it from the side table and put it back down to stretch my sore muscles. What the hell did I do last night that they still ache? Shouldn't they have healed overnight?

I guess it's just another question to ask the guys. Sometimes it sucks not knowing much about your new body. The guys are always patient, answering all the questions I have.

I get up to go pee, and once I'm done, I wash my hands and pick my phone back up, walking to the huge double door.

The sun shines through the glass, the warm sun rays lighting up my room. It looks like it's going to be a beautiful day in the Pacific Northwest. Finally, spring is here. The snow was nice, but I'm ready for some sunshine and the flowers to bloom.

I walk to the window and slide it open. The fresh crisp

air enters the room surrounding me. Maybe I'll go out for a run today.

"Don't you think that will be fun?" I talk to my wolf but she doesn't answer. I shrug, she must still be sleeping. I should let her sleep or she'll be grouchy and ruin this gorgeous day.

My heart is happy and full. I've finally found my kids. I've mated with my men. Everything is looking up for us.

That is until I find a message from an unknown number. *Not this again.*

My wolf doesn't try to stop me from opening it this time.

Usually when it's an unknown number, that means trouble, so although my wolf is still napping, I decide to leave it alone. I don't want anyone to ruin this day.

I quickly shower and grab the towels from the rack—one for my body and the other to dry my dripping wet hair. I go into the closet and bypass all of my jeans. I'm ready for summer. I pull out a sundress that sits above my knees. The top is yellow and the bottom is decorated with lemons. I grab my thin red belt and set it on top of my waist to complete my outfit.

I brush my hair with a comb as I stare at my violet eyes. They look glassy today. I can't really pinpoint what that means, and I'm not sure if I should worry, but I decide I'm not letting it ruin my day.

I walk downstairs. "Ava, Ezra!" I shout near the living room, but no one answers me. I should have checked their rooms before coming down here.

I don't see Lily anywhere, so I start on breakfast. The guys must have given her the day off.

Omelets for everyone. I grab the eggs from the fridge and a bowl and start to crack them before pulling out the other ingredients.

It takes longer than I anticipated. I forgot I had to cook for a lot of people now. Once I'm finished and have everyone's food on their plate, I look for my phone around the counter to call them, but I realize I've left it back in my room.

"Benji, Ash, Tyler, Az!" I shout from the kitchen, but no one comes down. They're all probably still sleeping. I clean up the mess in the kitchen and go back upstairs to get my phone. Maybe one of them texted me. I'm going to be pissed if they all went to breakfast without me, especially because I made them food.

I go to my kids' room first. Ezra's room is surprisingly clean—not a thing out of place.

That's strange.

I walk across the hall to Ava's room, stretching my aching arms. It didn't get any better while I was making breakfast. They're still sore. I thought by now the pain would go away.

I open Ava's door, and it is just as neat.

Where the hell did my kids go?

I try Ash's room, Tyler's, Benji's, and then Az's, but they're all empty. I try not to let the panic creep up.

There has to be an explanation for this, right?

"Wolf, Wolf!" I shout, but she doesn't answer back.

Am I dead?

I pinch my arm. Ouch! Fuck that hurt. Definitely still alive.

Am I in a parallel universe or something? Can that happen? Fuck, this type of supernatural shit is way out of my league. If I truly am, how the hell do I get back to my world? I shiver and push the thought about being stuck and never being found behind me.

I sprint downstairs and open the door, surprised it doesn't pull off the hinges by how hard I yank it.

I have no shoes on, and the grass against my feet feels real.

"Ezra, Ava!" I shout.

Nothing.

"Ash, Az, Benji, Tyler!" I yell out.

Nothing.

I swallow hard. The heat of the sun tries to warm up my very cold body. I haven't felt this cold since before I turned into a wolf.

I get on my knees, touching the soft texture of the vibrant grass. It's like I'm seeing the world in a whole new light again, the way I did when I turned into a wolf and my vision became sharper.

I walk back into my room and go to the dresser. My phone is right there. With shaky hands, I pick it up, but I drop the headphones that we're on the edge of the table.

I lower myself to pick them up and stand, staring at my violet eyes in the mirror before looking back at my phone. I click on the unknown message hoping it's from my kids or my guys. I need someone to tell me what the hell is going on.

Unknown: Kat, Wake the fuck up!

Huh? What does this shit even mean? I'm fucking *awake.*

I look in the mirror and my heart stops, two beads of red stare back at me. My mouth opens to scream, but my mouth gets covered.

I want to shriek in terror, and I would if I could, but I can't. I need to get myself out of here.

And go where? I think to myself. But that's a thought for later. Get somewhere away from this—whatever the fuck *this* is.

I push against the intruder trying to maneuver myself out of his grip. How did he get in here?

I step on his feet, but the invader picks me up. I touch the guy's face with my hands trying to grip at something, anything. I finally grab onto his hair and pull it back against me as hard as I can.

He lets out a loud cry and drops me. I have a chunk of deep black hair in my hand.

Someone else is in the room, but I can't quite see who it is.

"Wake up, Katarina!" The urgency in the tone has me opening the door to my room and sprinting out.

I grab my head, where the hell is that voice coming from, and why does it sound so muffled? I can't pinpoint who it belongs to.

I hear footsteps right behind me, but that isn't the scary part. The scariest part is knowing someone is watching me. It almost feels like this is a movie, and I'm the main character. It's like whoever this is can control what's going on in this moment. Is that even possible? I can't make out who it is and why they haven't shown their face.

I stumble down the stairs, sprinting through the foyer. I open the front door and take five steps from the porch, staring up at the night sky. No, it can't be.

Wasn't it sunny a couple minutes ago?

I don't have much time to investigate as the door opens. I don't wait. I don't know what the hell is going on, but one thing I know for sure is, I'm not letting red eyes catch me, and they're nothing like Silas's eyes. Where mine are violet, Silas's are red. This thing, whatever it is, isn't a vampire. The eyes look like huge red dots, at least from the small glance I was able to get.

I run as fast as I can through the forest. I try calling my wolf one more time, but she doesn't answer. It would be a lot faster if I could switch bodies.

The grass, branches, and dirt move beneath my feet as I speed up my pace. I miss dodging a bigger branch and fall on my face. I'm reminded of a horror movie where I'm the character about to get killed.

The intruder is only a couple of steps from reaching me. I struggle to stand up, but the body is already on top of me.

My eyes drift open, and I try to shield my eyes from the harsh light. My body is sweating and aching.

It was just a dream, and I try to convince myself to calm down from the panic.

The light in the room is bright. I quickly sit up and look around the room. It's decorated in violet just like my eyes.

Wh-What the fuck just happened? A tall man leaves the room. I don't recognize him, but he's gone before I can ask him what's going on.

My eyes find Ash as he stares at me. I think he was the one screaming my name to get me to wake up. Az is unconscious. Benji and Tyler are not here.

"Where are we?" My voice is horse and raw.

Images flood my mind of the gruesome and bloody scene we left behind.

"I don't know," Ash says, playing with the cuffs around his wrists.

"How did we end up here?"

"We were giving Benji time, but another supernatural took us by surprise. He took over our minds." He flicks his head to the door. He's quietly letting me know not to talk because someone is listening.

The knob starts to turn, and I drag my attention back to the door.

Oh no!

Fuck!

It's Theo.

I t's possible to live with someone for half of your life and not know a single thing about them; the man staring me down from the doorway is living proof.

"Kat." Theo walks into the bedroom with his perfectly tailored suit like nothing is wrong and he didn't just kidnap my kids.

My mouth is so parched, I try to lick my lips before asking, "Did you do something to me?"

"I had to get one of my guys to get into your head and trick you into believing that what was happening to you was real." I shiver at the thought of someone manipulating the images in my head. I'm getting a taste of my own power, and I don't like it.

"W-why?" I stutter and hate myself for it. "Why would you do that?" Knowing how easy it was for a stranger to invade the privacy of my mind makes me uncomfortable.

He shrugs without a care in the world. "To let you know that I can get into your head and make you see or feel whatever the fuck I want." The way he answers so nonchalantly irritates me. He wants to let me know that he holds all the power and I have none. It's exactly the sort of bullshit behavior I've come to expect from my ex-husband.

Since I became a shifter, the extreme temperatures don't bother me the same way they did when I was human, but now my whole body shivers and shakes like I'm standing in the middle of a blizzard with no clothes on. It's the same feeling I had in the dreamscape.

The man standing before me, the person I believed loved me, stares at me with the indifference of a perfect stranger.

"Where are *my* kids?" I ask as I grip the blanket tighter, grateful the cuffs are long enough for me to cover my body.

He ignores my question. "The kids you took from the facility?" he asks. His face turns angry for a single moment, but his mask slides back into place effortlessly, and he looks pleasant again. This is who I met at the diner for the first time when I was just a teen—the guy who made me feel like I was special.

I hate him.

My body is on edge and ready to pounce. If only I wasn't so fucking cold, I'd try to get out of these cuffs.

What the hell is going on with my body?

"It's the guy that left earlier. He's making you believe you're cold so you can't move," Ash answers my question without me having to voice it out loud. I hold onto my body tightly, wishing there was a heater in here to warm me up.

"Ava and Ezra are in the next room, Kat. If you cooperate, I'll let you see them." My teeth chatter loudly. I fucking hate this man with every bone in my body.

"W-why did you take them away from me?" I stutter. I hate this. I hate that I'm always so vulnerable when I'm around him. I hate that he always has the upper hand.

I watch as he smirks and makes his way to the bed. I try to scoot back but hit the back of the bed frame. There's nowhere to go.

Theo grabs his phone from his pocket and dials a number before bringing it to his ear. "You can let go of the power, Jace." One second I'm freezing, and the next, my body is back to normal.

I watch as he takes every confident step toward me as if he's already won this battle. I look over at Az. He's still passed the fuck out, and Ash is scrunching his forehead with so much force that it's like he's trying to fight something I can't see.

"Stay the fuck away from her, Theo," he spits Theo's name like it leaves a bad taste in his mouth.

Theo chuckles sinisterly as the hair on the back of my neck stands up. I've never seen this side of him before. Actually, I don't think I've ever seen the real Theo at all, and that's a very scary thought considering how long I lived with this man.

"I'll fry your brain," Ash says. Why doesn't he try it instead of talking about it? Did he get drugged? Is that why he's struggling?

"No you won't," Theo replies with confidence. "Remember, Ash, we're the ones who trained you four. We know all your strengths and . . . all your weaknesses."

I'm going to throw up.

The Iron Beast Pack without magic, the supernatural community knew these guys were scary—especially because of the training they had while working for the council. But now the person they worked for, the man who watched them closely, is here and unafraid of my guys.

He touches my face gently, and I'm repulsed by it, but thankfully he drops his hand. I once wanted his touch, craved it even, needed to be wanted by him. Yet he constantly gave me the cold shoulder.

"I'm going to kill you!" Ash makes an animalistic sound I've never heard, and I briefly look at him again. He's trying to push against some sort of block.

"Give it up, Ash. You can't use your powers," Theo says it like it's a matter of fact. "I've made sure of it." Then his body goes limp.

"What the hell did you do to him?" I screech in horror as Ash's head slumps forward to mirror Az.

"He wouldn't have let us talk, and I was tired of his yapping." He rolls his eyes in annoyance. "Let's just say, he took a little longer than his brother for the drugs to kick in." I don't like his tone. He's making me worry more about my guys.

My wolf has been so quiet through all this. She usually has something to say, even if it's only to bash someone. I believe she'd have so much to say about Theo—especially since she despises him.

"*Wolf.*" She doesn't respond, so I try again. "*Wolf.*" Still nothing. Where is she?

"If you're trying to communicate with your wolf, you

can't." I drag my glare back to Theo's dark eyes. How the hell did he know that's what I was trying to do? "No, I wasn't reading your mind, Kat. You were just concentrating very hard."

I stop breathing for a second. I gave him everything, my true self, and he gave me absolutely nothing. Well, except for my kids, but other than that, I don't know anything about the man in front of me.

"We've given you a shot." He points to my shoulder, and I look at it, but it looks just as smooth as ever. "It prevents you from shifting, contacting your wolf, or using your powers on me." Fuck! I think that's why my arm was hurting in whatever dream world I was in.

"If I was given a magic suppressant, how was your guy able to use his magic on me?" I ask.

"It prevents you from doing magic, but it doesn't prevent anyone else from using it on you." Double fuck!

"What did you do to Az?" My eyes flick to my other mate. I thought he'd wake up by now. I know he's still alive because his chest moves up and down, but I hate not being able to see those blue eyes of his.

He doesn't even glance at him, but his lip curls up in distaste. "They are both sedated. They'll wake up when I'm ready for them to be awake." I try not to show my slight relief. I'd rather they both be sedated then having their minds fucked with.

"Kat." He brings my attention back to him.

"Wh-what the hell do you want, Theo? Why did you marry me? Why did you go through all this trouble to put up appearances, make me believe you were normal, that the kids and I were normal?" I hate how my words sound like I'm pleading for him to give me an answer, but I'm exhausted from his games and truly need to know.

He had someone in his possession who has the same powers as me, but they are more experienced than I will probably ever be.

"Well, now that Benji's sister killed her," he says with an air of annoyance. "You'll fill her spot."

Uh, yeah, no. That's not fucking happening.

Again, I don't have to speak out loud for him to know what I'm thinking. "If you don't cooperate, I'll kill everyone you've ever loved." He spares a glance at the men slumped over behind him.

Theo will do it too. I don't doubt that.

"I've been watching you since the day Krissy tracked you to one of your foster homes. I haven't found anyone since you. I truly think you're the last one. We 'met' at the diner," he adds with air quotes to prove that this was all planned. "It didn't take much convincing to get you to marry me. You wanted the life I could provide. Then you gave me two children I never wanted. Maybe if I would've known your magic was hidden the whole time then I would have wanted them if they'd only prove useful, and now I found that they are. Well, at least Ava. I don't think . . ." he trails off before continuing. "I don't know about Ezra yet. He'll be a shifter for sure, but whether he gets any of your magic is still a mystery."

"Jess proved to be quite the con artist. She made me believe that your magic was gone. She kept you from the supernatural world. I didn't know she was a supernatural until recently. She was very good at hiding information." He chuckles before saying, "There were a few times that you almost caught me, but I played it off, and just like always, you believed me. I figured if you didn't know about it, you might accidentally let your magic slip."

I look at the small indents on my finger from our wedding rings that are still imprinted into my skin. I start putting things together.

"The rings were nothing more than—"

"A tracking device," he answers simply.

"That's the only reason you gave them to me? To track my location or to see if my powers sparked? You used them to keep me hostage." I hate that it took me this long to figure this all out. There was no way for me to know, but it's still a slap in the face. He's just as good as Jess was at hiding information from me.

"That day when you were attacked at the bar, I told Krissy not to pursue you, but she hated you so much. She was power hungry, but she was useful at the time. She helped me find you."

"She wanted me dead because I was a threat to her. She wanted my power for herself so that she could control you, and you knew you wouldn't have been able to control her, so you said all these pretty words to make her believe that she could take my power."

"Exactly," Theo says as he grabs his phone again, answering a message.

"But why didn't she take the other woman's power?" The other lady with violet eyes had the same power as I did. Except for one. I believe that's what she mentioned. Krissy could have had the ability to manipulate other supernaturals.

"Because I drained her too much. I had other—uses for her," he replies looking at his watch.

"Did you kill Jess?" He looks back up, putting it away. I already know the answer, but I need him to confirm. I need to see his face when he answers me.

"Yes." One word and zero remorse. "She was threatening my plans. She dug deep and found out who I was. I couldn't risk her talking to the wrong people, now could I? She had to die." Hearing those words coming from his mouth, I want to strip him of everything he has, his power, his control, his life. My best friend died because of him. The only friend who stuck with me from the beginning.

"Why didn't you tell me about this world?" I almost choke up again remembering the night I saw Jess's lifeless body on the floor.

"I was afraid that in telling you, I might spook you from manifesting your power. You were only supposed to be useful for one thing only, and that's to give me the power I needed." Of course it is. I shouldn't have expected anything else.

I still don't understand though. "Why go to this extreme to have the council at your fingertips?"

He opens his mouth to speak but then closes it as if thinking about his next words. "How is it fair that some shifters get to have power while others don't? I want to help the other shifters," he answers, and I would have believed him before all of this, but I know better now.

"You want to be able to have magic so that you can

control the supernatural community without having to rely on anyone else for power." He licks his lips, not denying anything I've said.

"You're right. That's why I told Krissy to kill her family, so she can gain more power, and in return, she'd give me what I was looking for." This is partly true. I can taste his words on my tongue, and I know he's being truthful. But—

"There's something more to this story, something you're leaving out on purpose. You don't give a shit about the council; you never have and you never will. You infiltrated them for a reason."

He chuckles darkly. "Oh, Kat. You know me too well." *No, I know nothing about you.* I'm starting to wonder if anyone does. I don't even think Krissy knew the *real* Theo.

"You wanted Krissy because she was able to prove that she could suck in all the witches' power. That's why you gave her that order and made her promises."

"Exactly. The day you caught me sleeping with her." I wait to see if the jealousy or the rage of that night hits, but I feel absolutely nothing. There's nothing I want from this man. "I never meant to let you go. But I couldn't choose your side now, could I? I needed her to keep trusting me so that she can keep looking for a way to transfer the power of the wolves' magic to me." And there it is, part of why he's doing this, but again, it's not the whole truth.

Fuck, I guess catching them in the act was a blessing. If I wasn't under the care of the guys then he would have eventually figured out that I had the power that Jess tried to hide from him all along.

"So, Krissy meant nothing to you? Just a means to an end?" I almost feel bad for her. She thought she was helping this lunatic out, and in return she was going to get more power. She sacrificed her family and gave her life to the man standing before me, and all he was doing was using her for an endgame that never included her.

"But there's more isn't there?" He shows me no emotion.

"You're not a shifter, you're—something else." I let the words out and exhale another wave of anxiety. He laughs and his eyes turn red. My body violently shakes, and it has nothing to do with the temperature.

This is what Ava is becoming.

I think the guys saw her eyes change color and wanted to figure this out before they told me. They're going to get an earful from me for keeping this shit a secret. I'll bring it up after we've beaten Theo and are all together as a family again.

"Your kind was wiped out of existence." My mind wanders back to Ava's school book.

He snarls, nothing like a wolf. His elongated claws are nothing like mine. They are pitch black and sharper than I've ever seen. The only place I ever saw this was in Ava's school book, and now she's like him.

Is my daughter going to be killed because of Theo?

Lycan. The name comes back to me.

That's what Theo is, what Ava is. Is Ezra going to be one too?

"If Ezra doesn't have your power, he'll most likely have

mine." I look at him baffled, and he laughs again. "You're just too transparent, Kat."

I need to school my features better.

"Ava doesn't have your power, but she has my ability, and she has—" he trails off in thought. "Something else. I want to confirm my suspicions before I say something." He looks at me again with a smile.

"How are you still alive if your kind was wiped out?" I wish he had been killed with the rest of them, but I'm quickly reminded that my kids wouldn't be here if it wasn't for him. I'm stuck in this situation of wishing he didn't exist and being grateful that my kids do.

He comes and sits next to me like we're truly a couple. How the hell does he manage to be at ease? I want to grab him and shred him to pieces, but when I'm pulled back, I'm quickly reminded that I have cuffs around my wrists.

"It's a very long story, Kat, but I'll give you the short version."

Finally, it looks like he'll answer the questions reeling in my brain. The truth will finally come out.

"I had a family before you, Kat. I had a mate and two boys." My mouth hangs open. This is not what I was expecting.

H oly fucking shit.

Never in a million years would I think those words would come out of his mouth. Theo has a whole family we never knew about.

I'm glad I found my real family because seeing the warm smile on his face as he thinks of another woman and the kids they had together would have killed me before. This is the first genuine emotion I've seen out of him my whole life.

"It ate me up when you had our kids. It felt like I was neglecting my own kids with Freyja." *Freyja*, he has never mentioned her name, not even in passing. This is the first I've heard of it. "It's why I told you I got a vasectomy. The guilt ate me up every day." I'd almost feel bad if he hadn't treated me like shit and experimented on the kids. "I said things to you that I know would make you feel bad because I hated myself for replacing my mate. In all the years before

I met you, I fucked other women, but I never had a relationship until you."

He pauses for a long moment, and just when I think that's the end of him sharing, he surprises me by starting back up again.

"We were at war. It was a gruesome battle, but we had the upper hand. The shifters wanted us out of this world, Kat. We were the ones being killed. We lived in harmony with the wolves until we were stabbed in the back. This was more than a thousand years ago." My eyes grow huge with surprise. No wonder this guy is a master manipulator. He's been alive longer than my mates, which is hard to believe because I thought my guys were pretty ancient. "I managed to escape before getting swallowed up in a hole."

"What a shame," I bite out, "that you didn't get sucked into the hole." But he just smiles and shakes his head.

"Your kind was hunted and killed too, and it wasn't because of lycans, it was the shifters." I must look shocked because he says, "Yeah the men you've taken a liking to." I try to swallow, but my mouth feels parched. "The council found out about me, wanted to make sure I was never able to bring my kind back."

"What the hell? So how were you able to join the council if they disliked your kind?" I'm going to need years of therapy to process all this information.

"Jess worked for the council for a while, but I didn't know anything about her. She was a seer, and she was able to plant information in their heads long before I showed up. She knew you'd be sought after and took precautions that helped ease the council, too bad she couldn't see her death," he says with a callus chuckle.

I wish my guys were aware of this.

When I know he isn't going to talk more, I ask, "What the fuck am I, Theo? You keep saying *my kind* like I'm supposed to know."

"You can manipulate other supernaturals the same way vampires manipulate humans, but you can also open a portal that my family is trapped in." Words of danger run through my mind, reminding me of what the woman with violet eyes said.

"N-no. That can't be right."

I regret asking. I don't want to hear anymore. I want to cover my ears, but the cuffs won't let me, and they swing back down on the bed.

"This is all true, Kat. In my lifetime, I've been able to capture three of your kind. The first one I captured killed herself immediately after she helped me infiltrate the council. For years I roamed this world until I found another one of your kind. The council was all mine—except for Silas. I never found out how he was able to not give in to your power. He's the only one I've found that can actually resist it. At first, he acted like he was enthralled and agreed to everything I said, but lately, he has led me to believe he has a plan of his own. I don't know what it is yet, but I'm going to find out."

I'm curious about Silas too, but I don't let him know that.

"The girl before you was weak. I've never met anyone

with so little power. The only thing she could do was sway people. That's when I knew I had to find a witch to help me." *Krissy.* "I figured I could take the powers of the wolves and use it for my gain, but she wasn't smart enough to figure out how to do that. I've seen and read ancient books of witches doing the craziest shit, and I know this would've been no different."

"Theo, what the hell is your plan?" I know he isn't telling me the whole truth.

"If you do this wrong you could die, Kat." He doesn't answer my question, instead, he gives me this vague, unsettling answer.

"What the fuck are you talking about, Theo?" I ask, my nerves and frustrations getting the best of me.

"You're going to open the portal, but if you do this wrong you could die, Kat." I swallow hard. I barely have knowledge on how to sway people and now I have to open a whole portal to a different dimension. "The council got rid of the lycans way before I took charge. It wasn't fair to your kind, but they didn't want anyone opening the portal to the werewolves because if it did, another massacre would happen, mainly the werewolves coming back for revenge." I open my mouth but then close it. He's definitely missing the part about other creatures roaming in.

"Rest up, Kat. We'll begin again tomorrow." He slumps forward. It's the first sign of exhaustion.

I'm almost afraid to ask. "So what are you going to do now?"

"I'm going to bring them back," he replies simply.

"That's why you need their powers, don't you?" It makes sense now. "This is why you tested on those kids. They were your last resort if I didn't have the power to open the portal. You wanted to see if you could harness enough power and use them to open the other side."

He smiles widely as he opens his arms. "Now we're going to be a happy family, Kat." This man has lost his marbles.

"If I would have known you'd give me kids with magical abilities, I wouldn't have stopped you from getting pregnant again." Oh fuck!

"No, Theo." That's not happening. "I don't want anything to do with you anymore."

"You don't have to be my wife," he says as if marriage is a ridiculous notion. I guess for him it is since in his world —our world—we have mates. Well some do. "But I'm not letting you and our kids go that easily." With that, he walks out of the room, leaving me with my mates who are still passed out.

My mind is running a thousand miles with so many thoughts. Anxiety is building up in the pit of my stomach.

"Kat." Az's voice is hoarse, and I immediately let go of my thoughts to focus on him.

"How do you feel?" My hands fidget with the handcuffs.

"I've been better." He tries to chuckle but starts coughing.

A minute later Ash opens his eyes. He scans the room until his eyes land on me.

"Where the fuck did he go?" Ash growls.

"He left," I say as I look at the door.

"What did he say to you?" Ash asks. Even though his harsh, urgent tone isn't directed at me, it's still frightening.

I slump back on the bed, wishing I were in mine, hiding underneath the blankets. "What didn't he tell me?" I answer, sounding more exhausted.

"Katarina," Ash sounds concerned, but when I don't look at him, he says more forcefully, "Katarina, look at me." My eyes immediately find his. "Whatever it is, we'll help you. We're your family, your mates, you don't have to do anything on your own anymore." The guys look at me with heat in their eyes, and I look at them the same way.

I smile kindly at him until I'm startled by a voice. "You guys better not get all sappy on me."

What the hell?

My eyes roam the room looking for the intruder.

The voice sounds familiar. "Show yourself." As if summoned, the girl we met at the facility steps out of the wall. What the hell?

"When did you sneak in?" Az asks.

"When Theo left." She rolls her eyes like that should be obvious.

"Why didn't you say anything before?" Az demands.

"I wanted to make sure we were the only ones here before I uttered a word." As she materializes in the violet room, her skin matches the violet covered walls. Within moments, her violet skin tone drains away, giving way to her natural brown pigment.

"I'm like a chameleon. I can adapt to my surroundings." That answers the question about how she had colored hair.

She comes over to me, searching her pockets until she pulls out a keychain full of keys. It takes her a couple tries before she's able to open my cuffs.

I rub my wrists while she helps untie my guys.

"We have to get my kids," I say urgently.

"Two guys are retrieving them now, Ryder and Cash," she replies.

"Fuck," Az mutters.

"Apparently they had their own vehicle and were keeping a safe distance from all of you guys. They're very stubborn. Your betas had to calm them down. Benji and Tyler looked like shit when they showed back up."

"Come on," she says as she opens the door.

"How did you guys find us?" I ask curiously.

"We can talk about that when we get out of here," she replies urgently.

"Should we check to make sure the kids are out?" I don't want to leave anything to chance.

"Oh, they're out," she answers confidently. "That's why Theo left to go find them. Cash and Ryder wasted no time."

Ash grumbles something about kids being careless under his breath.

"What's your name?" I ask the girl.

"Lina," she answers without saying anything more.

As soon as we leave the room, I notice we're not in the same facility we were in before. There is no blood or dead bodies lying on the floor. We're in a home I've never been in before.

"How's the security?"

"Tyler and his super-secret hacker guys got into it already." I look at her to see if she expands on that, but she doesn't.

"We trailed them. You guys have been here for almost twenty-four hours." How long was I in that dreamscape?

We walk down another corridor before she says, "Oh shit, it's the other way." We turn back around.

"Do you know where you're going?" Az asks with a hint of annoyance in his voice.

"Yes. Now shut up before you make me lose my concentration." Lina huffs, and I try not to chuckle at how defensive she sounds.

My heart thumps loudly. I don't want to get caught again. I wish more than ever that the shot they gave me will wear off soon. I need my wolf back.

She walks around the corner and back pedals, turning to us and putting her index finger over her lips, telling us to stay silent. We do as she says. There are footsteps echoing down the hall, but thankfully they are growing fainter as they pass. When it's silent, Lina gestures urgently, and we follow her to the back door on swift, quiet feet.

Lina eases it open, and we emerge out into the shadowy forest. The moment we're through, she begins to sprint, and my guys and I follow. Our legs take us further away from the house. We run until we find a road. Lina's head swivels in both directions before settling on the right. I hope she knows where she's going.

In the distance, engines rumble. My lungs burn and legs ache as I push myself faster. But it's no use, our pursuers are too quick.

Doors slam around us. Before I can react, rough hands seize me and drag my flailing body into the van. The engine surges and we peel away.

No. No! Did I seriously get kidnapped again?

They're not taking me without a fight. I start thrashing and clawing viciously at the arm locked around me. But as I look up, ready to kill my attacker, Tyler's handsome face appears above me instead. At the sight of him, the fight drains out of me. My body goes limp with relief as the engine roars and we leave.

Tyler's here. He came for me, and I'm safe now. I want to cry as I inhale his scent.

He takes notice of my pained expression and scrunches his brows. "Where do you hurt? Did anyone touch you?" he asks softly, but it's still more of a demand he expects me to answer.

"Physically, I can handle it, emotionally, fuck. I'm a mess of emotions I don't want to think about yet."

"We'll get through this together." I rest my head on his arm. I was trying to go for his shoulder, but he's too damn tall.

Someone ruffles my hair, and I already know it's Benji.

"You gave us a scare." He tries to sound humorous, but instead, his voice is strained.

I look around the van. "Where are my kids and your sister?"

"The kids are behind us." Benji moves his head so I can see the other vehicle trailing us. "My sister . . ." he sighs, and my heart speeds up. I know nothing good is going to come out of his lips. "She's stuck. She wasn't able to come."

"I'm so sorry, Benji. We'll find a way to get her out." Even though she looked at me in disgust, said I wasn't Benji's mate, and then tried to kill me.

"Where were we going with this again?" my wolf asks, and I'm relieved to hear her in my head again.

I glance down at my hands, seeing my talons come out just to reassure me that my wolf is really there—talons that look so different than Theo's and my daughter's.

"You want to know where we are going with this? We're absolutely going to help out Benji's sister," I reply.

When we get out of the van, I immediately wait for my kids in front of theirs. As soon as I see Ezra's head poking through the door, I run to their vehicle. When both of his feet hit the ground, I rush in for a hug.

"I missed you," I murmur in his ear.

"I missed you too," he says right back, hugging me just a little tighter.

"Hey, Mom," Ava says, standing next to her brother. I move to her next, giving her a tight hug.

"It looks like we're going to have more students," she says as we pull apart.

"Where are they?" Ryder comes up to us smiling, but his eyes still look strained as if he's worried that another threat is approaching. I hate to see that look on a teenage kid. They should be having fun, not waiting for the next threat to take us out.

"They've already settled in their rooms," Ryder answers.

"I'm tired, Mom," Ava says as her head hangs low.

"So am I," Ezra agrees.

The kids say their goodbyes and rush back to the house.

My body is exhausted by the time I walk inside. I feel like I've been up for days, and the nightmare dreamscape I was in really took a toll on my body and mind.

I drag my heavy feet up the stairs to my room, but before opening the door, Az grabs my elbow to stop me, and I look up at him with concern.

"What's going on?" I am hesitant about taking another step. I'm so on edge that I automatically think someone is here to attack.

"Relax, Kat. We're taking you there." He points to a closed door that's next to mine. I've actually never been there before. We walk together to the room, but just before I get there, I stop.

"Let me go get some clothes." I try to walk back but he stops me.

"We have everything you need in there." He opens the room, and my curiosity propels me forward.

Woah. This room is bigger than mine, but what catches my attention is the huge bed sitting right in the middle of the room.

"So umm . . ." I scratch the back of my head nervously.

"We're all sleeping in here," Ash says from right behind me. I've slept with each of them but never with all of them at once. I'm starting to get a little nervous about the idea of having my men all in the same room together and naked.

The red and black sheets remind me of Az's room. Actually, this looks like it would be Az's room with all the toys and ropes stored neatly on one side of the wall. I look up to see hooks. This is like Az and Ash's room put together.

Then I see a camera in the corner of the room. "Why is there a camera in here?"

"Just in case I want to watch later," Tyler says as he walks past me, winking and pulling his shirt off on his way to the shower in the next room.

I look around to see if I can spot anything that belongs to Benji. "I'm in charge of music," he says as he walks past me, looking down at his phone just as music bursts from hidden speakers.

"We don't have to do anything tonight," Ash whispers in my ear. "I know you're tired." I truly want this. I need to forget everything that Theo just told me. I need to get him out of my head. I want to focus on my guys and nothing else.

"I need a shower," I say, looking down at the clothes

I'm wearing that are sticking to my sweaty skin. I need this all off.

"It's right in there." Ash points to the room Tyler disappeared into.

Without noticing, my legs start moving in the direction Ash pointed. The door is slightly open, and I push it forward, letting the door hit the stopper with a bang.

I walk into a spacious bathroom that has a shower and a bath.

Tyler is already inside the steamy shower, so I peel off my dirty clothes with each step toward him until I'm pushing the foggy glass door open and stepping in behind him. Wrapping my arms around his hardened frame, I pepper kisses along his muscled back.

"Why do you have cameras in the bathroom?" I murmur.

"Because I'm a kinky motherfucker who wants to watch his mate fuck four guys on the big screen whenever I want." I don't have to look at him to know he's smiling.

I laugh, and for the first time in a while, my body is relaxed. I'm going to enjoy this moment. I deserve it—we all deserve it.

"So . . . you want a sex video?"

"Pretty much." He doesn't try to deny it. I love his raw honesty. It turns me on knowing my mate wants to watch me fuck his brothers.

I lower my arms down his leg and they drift to the center. I find what I'm looking for, and he groans as I pump his length in slow, lazy movements. Up and down I stroke as he follows the rhythm of my hand.

"There you are, little brat." The door to the shower opens and closes.

Az grabs me by the neck, taking me by surprise. I let go of Tyler as Az pins me against the tile. "Remember we agreed, Tyler, no coming until Kat has."

Tyler mumbles incoherently, and he sounds annoyed. I want to laugh about Az ruining the orgasm Tyler could've had, but Az has a tight hold on me, cutting off my air supply.

"Let's give this brat right here a proper orgasm," Az says as his sharp nails puncture my skin, and I feel warm liquid trailing down my throat and onto my body.

"I like that idea brother." Tyler lowers his body. I can't see him anymore since Az has me pinned to the wall.

Tyler adjusts my feet onto his shoulder. The anticipation of him eating my pussy has my body pumping with so much adrenaline.

I want to tell Tyler that he shouldn't leave me hanging, but I can't talk. Before I can get anymore impatient, my body trembles as Tyler glides up and down my clit. My body is wet and ready for him. He runs his tongue over my pussy slowly, and it's almost painful. I want him to speed up. I want to climax with his mouth on me.

With his other hand, Az runs his thumb across my hardened nipple. He hovers close, takes one look at me, and puts it in his mouth, biting down hard enough to draw blood again.

The pain and pleasure rockets through me, and I scream out, wanting so much more. All I can think of is my need to ride Az's dick while he bites my tits, but I want

Tyler to lick me harder and faster at the same time. That's when Tyler slides a finger in my pussy.

"Does it feel good, little brat." That's when I notice Az is not playing with my breasts. He must have seen the look of disappointment because he laughs darkly and goes back to my nipples.

I close my eyes tightly as Tyler picks up speed. He sucks on my nub and I melt. If Az wasn't holding me up with his hand on my neck, I'd have already fallen to the floor. That's how weak my legs are.

"Open your eyes." Az bites my earlobe, prompting me to do as he says. "I want to see you as you come undone."

My short supply of air, the heat of the moment, and the steam from the hot shower are making me lightheaded.

"How does she taste?" Az asks Tyler as I'm panting close to an orgasm.

"So sweet," he mumbles. "I never knew how amazing she'd taste covered in blood." His response on how good I taste is all I needed to hear to be put over the edge. I scream, not caring if the guys outside in the room can hear me.

My body is worn. Az removes his hand from my neck and Tyler is there to catch me.

I stand on shaky legs. "I came in here to shower, but my body is spent." I walk toward the shower head, letting the hot water drip down my hair.

"That's why we're here to help you," Az says as he grabs the shampoo from a built-in shelf I wasn't aware was even there.

The lavender scent calms my mind as he massages the shampoo into my scalp. I rinse my hair and he grabs the conditioner. This one smells like vanilla, and the combination of the two is heavenly.

As Az works on my hair, Tyler delicately runs the soapy sponge all over my body to clean me up.

I get underneath the shower head as the water washes away the soap and conditioner.

Once I'm done, I move to the side to let them have their turns. "No, stay there," Tyler says as he turns another knob and a second shower head starts to pour water. Az and Ash take turns underneath it until they've finally finished.

"You're done already?" Benji asks as he grabs a towel from the rack covering me. "I'll be quick, Kitty Kat," he says as he walks into the shower.

"You were too slow," Az says to him trying to get a rise out of Benji.

"Fuck off Az." Az chuckles and leaves the bathroom.

I walk next to Tyler. I dry off my hair and my body. Once done Ash walks in, in nothing more than a pair of sweats.

"You need help wiping the drool off your face, Kat?" I close my mouth and smile shyly.

"Tyler, if my mate wants to look at me like she wants to devour me, I'm completely fine with it," Ash replies.

I try to change the conversation, but I don't think it's any better. "So umm . . . how do we mate?" I use the towel to dry off my hair to give me something to do because my hands are starting to shake. Is it going to hurt, feel good, will I feel anything at all? The unknown part is terrifying.

"All you have to do is lay back and enjoy. You think you can do that?" Fuck yeah I can.

"Uh, yeah," I say, fisting the towel harder, but now my legs start to tremble.

I'm surprised my wolf hasn't come out yet, I checked in with her, but she's satisfied and excited with what's about to happen.

Tyler turns me around, and with his lips against mine he murmurs, "My wolf recognized you from the beginning. Wanted us to mate with you. I didn't think it was possible." For some reason, I can feel how content my wolf is with those words. Maybe these wolves inside of us have a deeper connection to mating that my human side can't comprehend.

"Come here." Ash grabs my chin, pulling my gaze away from Tyler. He holds on until we stop walking. We end up right in front of the bed.

My eyes flit around the room nervously, looking anywhere but at the white-haired god. With his other hand, he rakes his fingers through my wet hair.

"Kneel." I do as he asks and get on the floor. He leaves and goes into the bathroom. When he comes back, he has an extension cord and a blow dryer.

What the hell does he need an extension cord for?

He plugs the extension into the wall and then plugs in the blow dryer. He holds the unit like a gun, and I want to laugh at how menacing he looks.

He sits in the middle of the bed and turns it on. The warm air blows around my strands as he runs his fingers from my scalp to the tip of my hair. A wave of tingles runs down my back, relaxing me further into his hands.

"Does it feel good?" Ash asks.

"Mhmm . . ." is my response as he continues to blow dry my hair.

Once it's no longer wet, Ash turns it off and I pout. That was really relaxing.

"Don't worry, Kat," he says as he unplugs the dryer. "We're just getting started."

"Stay on your knees," Ash demands as I attempt to get up, and my body obeys.

I look up to him for further directions. "Tyler, do you want to get your cock sucked first?" I try to glance at Tyler, but Ash grabs my chin. "You look at me, Kat."

Someone from behind me grabs my wrists, binding them together. I immediately smell Az. He ties the soft rope around my hands. "Only mouth no hands." I nod my head.

Tyler's cock blocks my face. He wipes the precum on my lips. I stick out my tongue and lick the salty liquid. I start at the base of his cock and lick all the way to the tip, he groans loudly.

Benji is in the corner playing with his length. I've just realized that I have them all here together. They're all watching me, and it feels exhilarating.

The sight of them motivates me to keep going. I swirl my tongue on his slit, more salty liquid gets on my tongue and I lap it all up.

Someone grabs my head and massages my scalp with their fingers.I quickly recognize those hands as Ash's.

"That's it, baby, take him all in." He starts to slow as my mouth adjusts to his length. Once I've pumped it a few times, Ash fists my head, and Tyler slams his cock down my throat. Tears stream down my face as it becomes harder to breathe. With his other hand, Ash wipes them off quickly before Tyler's dick slams the back of my throat.

One moment, I'm taking him all in, and the next, he's pulling out completely. I look up at Tyler confused. He gently runs his fingers down my cheek and says, "You almost made me come, but we want to wait until we all do it together."

"My turn," Benji shouts eagerly. My eyes find him, and he stares at me with heat, his playful mood gone, replaced by need.

"Open nice and wide for Benji," Ash murmurs in my ear.

When Benji stands in front of me, I open my mouth, and he shoves his shaft down my throat. I'm actually surprised he's going fast. I thought he'd start off by going slow. "See what you're doing to him." Ash lets go of my head. "You're driving him mad."

In the distance, I hear some shuffling, and I think Ash and Az are preparing for whatever comes next. I have no clue what it is, but I trust my men completely.

"Move your knees wider." I adjust as Benji caresses my face, the soft sensation completely opposite of the rough way he's pumping into me. It's less than what I just did with Tyler. "Wider," he says as he taps my knees with his bare feet, showing me what he wants. "That's it, little brat," Az whispers in my ear.

I hear a bottle opening up, and a few seconds later, he uses the lube to cover my ass. I know what's coming and I want it.

The cold metal toy slides in and out, and I moan into Benji's cock. I close my eyes, loving the sensation. I'm sucking harder and moaning louder, and the next thing I know, Benji slides completely out with a pop sound.

"Fuck, Kitty Kat, you almost had me coming in the back of your throat." Benji gets on his knees, and with two fingers, he pumps in and out of me. "You're so drenched and ready for us, aren't you?"

I moan in response. I can't even think straight right now. All I can think about is what's pumping in and out of me. Benji and Az make sure I don't fall over. Az holds the ropes that bind my hands and Benji fists my hair.

"I want that nice and stretched for when Benji takes you down there." Fuck I can't wait. This is pure bliss.

Az finally leaves the toy inside and Benji removes his hands, leaving me cold and wanting more. I glower.

"Don't pout, love," Tyler says as he watches me with heat in his eyes. "We're not finished yet."

Az pulls me up and unties me. I shake my hands as the blood rushes back. "Lay in bed," Ash orders. I ease onto my back, facing the ceiling. I can see my naked form in the mirrors above. My gaze slides to one of the cameras flashing red.

Ash grabs my cheeks with one hand and has me facing him. "You can watch later, but for now, we're going to cover your eyes." Az hands him a red cloth that looks like his usual handkerchief, and everything is dark once he covers my eyes.

"What's your color?" Ash asks.

"Green," I respond.

"That's my girl," Benji says, and I can hear his smile.

My senses are hyper aware since I have the blindfold now. Something is wrapped around my wrists, probably cuffs. They take my arms, and I hear a clicking sound. Next, they grab my legs and stretch them out, leaving me exposed to them. I hear another snap. I try moving my hands and legs, but they won't budge. I'm tightly secured and at their mercy.

Something light and fluffy like a feather is dragged against my nipples. I arch my back, wanting to feel more of it, when something clamps on my nipples. It's a sharp pain as the feather circles my breast.

"You look fucking sexy, Kat," Ash whispers against my lips as he kisses me. He rubs his chest against the clamps, and I gasp at how sensitive they feel.

He pulls away. "We've got another surprise." Az's dark voice rings in my ears.

A sudden intrusion in my pussy causes me to gasp, and the gentle vibrations tease me. Someone removes the clamps, letting the blood rush back to my breasts and making them feel delicate.

A suction is added to each of my nipples. The fluttering tongue inside the suction cup vibrates, making my tits harden more than they were before.

Everything in my body is sensitive. I don't want this to

end. I can feel it building up low in my core. "I'm going to come," I growl.

My pleasure is heightened, I move my pelvis back and forth to chase the orgasm.

When I come back down from the high, my body becomes hyper aware of everything that's vibrating.

The suctions are removed from my body. My body misses the toys, but I'm relieved when they are pulled away.

Az takes off the cloth, and I'm surprised to see a dimly lit room. I thought for sure I was going to get assaulted by the harsh light.

Benji undoes my wrist restraints while Az undoes my ankles. "Alright, Kat, I'm going to lift you up," Benji says as he gently places himself underneath me. My body still craves more pleasure.

Benji runs his hands down my belly and behind my ass where he pulls out the toy and hands it to Az. I don't pay attention to what happens because my focus is on Benji as he trails kisses down my neck, making me shiver in pleasure.

Tyler positions himself in the front while Az's legs are around my neck. I lick my lips looking at his pierced cock, and he grunts. Ash is next to Az.

"Alright, Kitty Kat," Benji says as he slides his length down my ass. I close my eyes, but Ash slaps my face. "Open them," he demands. This is all so sexual that I don't get mad about the slap.

Once Benji and I have our rhythm going, Tyler slips right in, grunting in satisfaction. He pumps in and out before he starts to play with my clit.

Az doesn't need any prompting. He runs his talons down my neck, creating a trail of blood seeping from the wounds, and I gasp as he inserts his cock down my throat. I'm so full I don't know where Ash fits in.

I don't have to guess too long before he grabs my hand in his. I fist his dick as my other mates pump all three of my holes.

I'm so sensitive everywhere, but my body craves more, and they deliver by quickening their pace.

There's so much pleasure that I don't know if I can contain it all in my body as it wants to unleash itself. Once I know that I no longer can, my orgasm starts to build up. I want to tell them, but I have Az's cock hitting the back of my throat. I whimper.

"Shh . . . just hold it a little while longer." I want to tell him that I don't think I can. I'm about to burst.

Az grabs my other hand, running his talons up and down like a caress, but blood gushes out.

Finally when their dicks begin to expand, they all bite a part of my body. Az my wrist, Ash my neck, Benji my shoulder, and Tyler the side of my breast.

That's when I feel the magic intertwining each of us together. It weaves into my heart like there have always been four pieces missing, but now it's fully complete. As we become one, our orgasms explode and we howl.

We pant with exhaustion. When we come down from the pleasure we lie limply in bed.

The next thing I know, I'm in a bath and my body is being washed, but I'm too tired to open my eyes. My heart is content. I faintly hear them in my head, and I say to each of them I love you and they reciprocate my words. My heart is filled with the joy and happiness I haven't felt in a long time, and my body drifts off into a slumber.

They're still sleeping in bed when my eyes drift open, and I move carefully between Ash and Tyler trying to get out of their comfort.

After all that sex my body is craving water. I go to my drawer and pull out a violet nightgown, and I have no doubt this was something Tyler picked out for me. He has impeccable taste in clothing.

As I slip the soft nightgown over my head, my eyes fall to The Kiss of Death tucked away in the bottom of the drawer, but the item next to it grabs my attention. It's a sparkly violet leg strap with white gemstones across the band. With excitement coursing through me, I can't wait, so I try it on, loving the way it looks and feels.

I put my weapon inside the holder to test the weight of wearing it, and when I open the door, the guys still don't stir. They're probably as exhausted as I am. After getting my water, I'm coming back up and snuggling with all of them. The bite marks all over my body still ache, but they're a reminder that we are now whole. It's something I never knew I was missing.

I get to the kitchen and grab a glass then go to the fridge and press the button for water and slide it in. As I tip the glass against my lips and let the cool liquid run down my throat to my belly, a voice behind me makes my stomach drop.

"Kat." I gasp and immediately turn around, not expecting a whole gang of people in the kitchen. How did I miss them when I walked in? "Stay where you are."

"What the—"

"We're with the council, and you're under arrest." My glass falls to the floor and shatters, and in my head, I can feel my men stir awake.

I knew it was coming. I just didn't think it would be so soon. I thought I'd have more time with my kids and my mates.

"What's going on?" Ash asks in my head, startling me. Having them in my mind will take some time to get used to.

The fast and rough steps the guys make are loud enough to shake the house.

An entire army swarms through the kitchen and probably extends into the living room and outside.

My guys push through to get to me, but as soon as they part the crowd in the kitchen, their limp bodies fall to the floor.

Theo was not going to let me go that easily. I'm too important to his mission to bring back the lycans. To bring back his—*other family.*

At least now I know the real reason he needed my power.

If I could use my powers to persuade them, I would, but they're all wearing shades. It's like they've done this before, and they probably have. They've been alive for a very long time.

I look at my men lying on the floor. What the hell is going on with them? Their eyes are closed, but I can see movement behind their heavy lids as if they were stuck in a bad dream. I try to call out to them, but it's like the mind connection we have is closed. We can't communicate with one another.

I look up to see a guy with a tattoo on his forehead looking bored out of his mind, but his unwavering gaze is focused on the guys. He has to be the one doing this to my men.

"Once she leaves with us, you can lose your grip on your power." The man with the tattooed face nods his head without uttering a single word.

My eyes dart between my men with fear and confusion. Their muscles tick and twitch, but they can't seem to wake up or move. They don't know what's happening to them. I shiver remembering the dreamscape I was in. It must be like that.

My men fight against whatever force they are facing, and their lips turn a sickening shade of purple.

"Ash, wake up!" I yell, my voice trembling with uncertainty. He stops twitching for a moment like he hears me, but then his struggle continues.

"Tyler, wake up!" I shout louder, but there is still nothing.

"Az, wake up. I need you!" He stirs desperately in his

sleep to reach me, but he can't fight the power that's keeping him under.

"Az, it's not real, whatever you're facing, it's not real." My voice breaks. He seems to be struggling the most with whatever is going on in his head. His claws come out of his fingertips, and he's dragging them across the marble floor, making long, sharp dents like he's trying to escape.

Though I'm worried about all my guys, Az and Ash are the ones I'm most anxious for. They told me about their past lives before we mated to make sure I really wanted to be with them, but of course I wanted them. Their past doesn't change anything.

"Make it stop," I whisper, watching my broken mate struggle against whatever he believes is real.

"We'll make it stop when you come with us, and we'll leave your family alone," one of the intruders replies. I don't look up to see who it is because I don't care.

A tear falls down my cheek and onto the floor. This will probably be the last memory I have of them. But I remember what we did last night, and a small smile shapes my lips, but it's gone quickly.

I take a deep breath before saying my next words. "I'll go with you." I can't look at them anymore. It's going to kill me to see their faces.

I'm already out the door when I hear another man saying, "Let them go."

The screaming and the shouting begin, but I have too many supes surrounding me for them to notice me or for me to be able to see them.

At least we had a beautiful night together. The only

thing I regret is not being able to say goodbye, but I know my guys will take care of my children as if they were their own.

Now I know what Krissy meant by, *"He will take you, and your men won't be able to protect you."* She was talking about Theo.

I can almost taste the sisters' words now. *"It's a shame that it had to fall on you. Especially because you have kids."* Did they foresee this happening?

All of this because I got bitten by fucking Dan, but it feels like everything was supposed to happen this way. The magic I was born with would have stayed dormant my entire life if it wasn't for the magic of being a wolf, and without becoming a wolf, I wouldn't have found my true mates.

A pang of guilt shoots through me as I let my mind linger on my guys. They've all been through so much pain and loss, and they don't deserve to be abandoned this way. We haven't had much time together, but the kids and I have quickly become their whole world. I know I'm letting them down by going quietly, and as I'm saving them from death, I'm also condemning them to a lifetime of regret.

Maybe I ignored the sisters' warning all this time because I never understood the full magnitude of what they were telling me. I was too fixated on my guys being larger than life and more dangerous than any threat that we could face. I was so wrong.

I don't know if I'll make it out of this alive, but I know one thing for sure: I'm taking Theo down with me. I can't let myself open the portal. If there was a reason for it to be closed then whatever is on the other side shouldn't be let out.

Someone grabs my wrists and holds them together, binding them behind my back. I follow his instructions, trying to ignore the sharp pain that makes it hard to wiggle my fingers. I see a big needle heading for my shoulder, and as soon as it punctures my skin, my body grows cold.

They're numbing my power.

We walk down the porch stairs with the dark sky starting to lighten. A van is waiting for me ominously in the distance.

I look to my right and stumble back a step, but I'm pushed forward.

"Mom!" Ava shouts before she's shoved into the vehicle. I push myself toward the group of people surrounding me, but it's no use. They're not letting me go anywhere. This wasn't part of the deal. If I agreed to go with them, they were going to stop hurting my guys and leave my family peacefully.

I try to find Ezra in the crowd, but it doesn't look like they have him. I don't see him anywhere, but I'm not sure if that's a good thing. What if he fought back like the guys? What if he's hurt, or what if he's—No. I can't think like that!

"Let my daughter go!" I howl, but no one responds, and instead I am pushed forward roughly.

The ride to wherever we're going is silent. I have a bag over my head, so I try to memorize the movements, but it's no use. There were too many turns, and I think it was done on purpose.

"You know he's a werewolf, right?" I try to see if anyone can reason with him, but they all laugh it off. "He is. He's playing all of you guys. He's trying to get me to open the portal."

More laughter.

That's when I decide to give up and keep my mouth shut. The other violet voyager did a great job in making them believe what Theo wanted them to.

The vehicle finally stops. They rip the cover from my face and I gasp, the crisp night air filling my lungs. I blink against the glare of the full moon overhead. We're surrounded by dense forest, the smell of pine and wet earth is strong.

I'm pushed toward a four-wheeler, a really nice Polaris.

"So, I'm guessing this isn't our stop," my wolf groans.

"I guess not," is the only response I have for her.

"Get on," one of my masked captors orders. Their dark sunglasses give no glimpse of their eyes, eliminating any chance of swaying them.

Before I can react and try to escape, a sharp pain stabs my neck. The tranquilizer spreads through my veins, the forest spinning away as darkness consumes my vision. My body goes limp, slumping forward. Strong arms catch me, draping me over the four-wheeler seat like a rag doll. My head bounces with each bump and jolt as we set off again.

The four-wheeler kicks up choking clouds of dust that sting my eyes and coat my lips with grit. I try to lift my head, to call out, but the sedative still floods my system, leaving me limp and mute. I can do nothing except watch the spinning earth, completely powerless.

Sometime later, I open my eyes to see the ground racing by below, my limbs dangling weakly. I drift back to semi-consciousness as I'm dragged down a dirt path. I notice how pitch black it is away from the city. The moon overhead provides the only illumination. My weakened muscles barely respond, but I manage to summon my wolf vision. The path leaps into clarity, each tree and leaf vivid to my enhanced eyes. Though the sedative still courses through me, at least I can now see clearly through the eerie darkness that surrounds me. For now, all I can do is stumble along as my captors pull me deeper into the shadows.

The men holding my arms walk me to the center of a small clearing surrounded by tall trees. There are chairs lined up in a circle around us.

"This is where we're meeting the council?" I ask, knowing full well that this was not for the council at all. This is for Theo. He just made everyone believe it was. He's good that way, making people believe him.

I honestly thought it would be in an elaborate building.

As if I summoned them, a group of people started to show up. They all wear sunglasses so I can't look at their eyes directly. At first, they seem to materialize directly from the dark forest. But as more join the circle, my eyes catch on shapes lurking deeper among the trees. Partly obscured by brush is a group of ATVs. That explains the sudden gathering. The vehicles allowed swift, quiet transport through the woods.

"So it is true, she does have violet eyes," says a male standing right in front of me. I want to shift uncomfortably, but my wolf doesn't let me.

"I thought we got rid of all of them," a lady says from behind me.

"I'm sorry you had to live with that," another lady with pointed ears voices, looking at me with disgust. She has to be Fae. I've read in the kids' school books that Fae are exceptionally beautiful but equally cruel. The sneer on her delicate face gives her away—and the man next to her as well.

I look at the rest of the council members, but Silas is nowhere to be found. I wonder if they killed him because he lied to them about me.

"I don't think so. He's a smart man," my wolf replies, and I breathe in relief when I hear her in my mind. My wolf wasn't lost when they numbed my powers, and she's right, Silas isn't one to be captured, and if by the off chance he was, he wouldn't have gone down easily. All these people would've had some type of injury. As it stands right now, everyone looks perfect and nothing seems out of place.

Everyone here believes they'll be watching my death. What they don't know is that Theo is the real threat in this scenario. They all fall in line because of him, he's been pulling strings since he captured my kind.

"Welcome council members. I'm glad you were all able to come on short notice." I follow the sound of Theo's voice to his smug face on the other side of the clearing, and

I try to suppress the nausea rolling through my stomach. Everyone starts to make their way to the chairs. Some stare directly at me and some act as if I don't exist.

I'd be lying if I said I wasn't nervous about what's to come.

Theo looks around and frowns before putting on that huge fake smile of his. I'm surprised he switched his expensive suit for something sportier. He's wearing sweats and is shirtless.

My biggest concern is what will happen if they find out my daughter is a werewolf. Theo's been around for a long time, they trust him, and I can't trust that man to protect my daughter.

Is that what Silas was trying to tell me about Ava, that she was the cursed one? Was he actually trying to protect her? Did he know she was a werewolf?

Chapter 29

Kat

Where's Ava?

I don't know whether to feel relieved or afraid that I can't find her anywhere. If she's here, that means Theo will be using her for his plan, but if she isn't, I don't know what these men have done with her.

I briefly look at Theo, and he gives a chilling smile that does nothing to alleviate my nerves. He's got something up his sleeve, and I know that I won't like anything he has planned.

"The prophecy states that the woman who gets bit and turns will destroy us," Theo informs them, but they know exactly what he's talking about.

So that's the reason I was being hunted and why shifters weren't allowed to turn anyone. They were trying to protect their power and themselves. The fact that I have violet eyes just seals the deal for my fate.

"But that isn't why we're here today." As soon as those

words leave his mouth, the mood changes and the council members shift uncomfortably.

"What do you mean?" the vampire asks, the seat next to her is still empty—Silas's seat.

"Detra, where's Silas?" Theo asks instead.

"How should I know?" Detra responds. "I don't watch his whereabouts." The lady sounds irritated, and I briefly wonder if Silas and her have bad blood between them.

Theo's posture doesn't change, but I have a slight feeling that he's annoyed with her response.

"Too bad." Theo rubs his chin in thought, and I wish I knew what he was thinking.

"You already know," I tell myself, knowing that's what my wolf would've said if our connection wasn't numbed.

He intends to kill them all; he wishes Silas was here so he can do the same. He only kept them alive because they were useful to his plans, and now it looks like they're no longer needed, and that's when the lycan will strike.

He clears his throat before he begins again. "As I was saying, we're not here for the reason you all think." They look at each other baffled. I don't know how Theo is going to control the council plus their bodyguards unless he has another purple-eyed woman like me he's holding hostage somewhere and they all decide to take off their sunglasses.

"Theo, I know she is—was—your wife, but she's a threat to us." The Faerie woman looks at her peers like they'll side with her and not Theo.

Then it dawns on me, she actually thinks that Theo is having a change of heart because I was his former wife.

These people really don't know shit about what's going on. They're all fucking clueless.

"Actually, Aisling, it has nothing to do with that at all." My heart races. Will he tell them the truth or will he strike first? Theo will want them to know before he kills them. I'm sure that he could have easily killed them without them knowing, he's just putting on a show now.

"What the hell are you getting at Theo?" the shifter woman asks. She looks annoyed that she has to be here. "Because, if we didn't come to kill her then why are we here?"

"Even if she didn't get turned, we still have to kill her because she can open the portal where our ancestors have locked up the werewolves." The male Fae speaks up for the first time. I want to argue my case and tell them that I actually have no clue how to do that. That I just got my powers recently.

"And with good reason." I don't turn to see who spoke. All my attention is on Theo because he looks suspicious. He's about to unleash something on them.

"You should punish Theo alongside her. Isn't that right, Julian." Aisling looks at the Fae seated next to her. She doesn't try to say my name, which should irritate me, but it doesn't. I have other concerns—like watching Theo very closely to see if I can spot his next move. "You should've come forward as soon as you found out information on your ex-wife." They argue with one another about what should've been done instead.

This is my chance to escape. While they're all occupied bickering with one another, I look around to see if I can find an escape, but there's too many guards standing behind the council members for me to do anything and the sedative I was given has only just begun to fade.

"Don't you see, Theo? She's the mate to the Iron Beast Pack. If we don't kill her then they'll be too powerful to stop, and they'll rule over the wolves. Do you really want that, Theo?" The shifter's eyes gaze toward me, and I shift uneasily under their scrutiny. "We have to do it now before they find her and destroy us all."

"She's not their mate, their *mate* died," Theo says with confidence.

I stand very still, trying not to make a move. I think I've forgotten how to breathe by how tightly I'm holding onto my breath.

I'm shocked that he didn't guess that part. He really did think the woman he had locked up was their mate. Explains why Zoe was so certain that I wasn't their mate. I can't really fault her for that one, after all, she was locked up because of Theo, and she didn't know any better. Theo was her only source of information.

Please don't ask me, please don't ask me. I repeat it over and over hoping he moves on.

Theo faces me again, shit. He's frowning now. "Kat," I hate the way he says my name. "Is this true?" he asks, trying to confirm what the shifter voiced.

There's no point in lying, he'll see right through it.

"Yes." As soon as those words come out of my lips, I try to see if I can reach my mates, but our mind link is still not there.

As if it doesn't faze him, he turns back to the council. "Bring Ava out."

My body trembles in fear. "Theo, please," I whisper, hating that I have to plead with him not to harm our daughter, but I'd do anything to protect her. "Leave her out of this." He's still staring out into the open. "She doesn't have *my* magic." He turns to me then and gives me a wide smile, showing me his bright white teeth.

He looks behind him and nods, then he looks at me again. "While Krissy's magic was looking for a host, it found Ava to attach itself to."

Shit.

<h2 style="text-align:center">Chapter 30</h2>

<h3 style="text-align:center">Tyler</h3>

It's been hours since the council members took Kat and Ava. Although our connection is temporarily numb, I know that she hasn't been killed. I only know this because we would feel the pain in our hearts of our missing soulmate.

I'm not sure where they took her. They covered their scent so we can't track them, and it's a struggle not to tear this place down in anger. The old Tyler is slowly creeping up, and I'm fine with it. I need to be ruthless.

The house is too quiet.

Once the trucks left, the rest of the guards were here for an hour before they let us all go. While we were under the dreamscape they shot us with sedatives to numb our power and connection. We were helpless for a few hours. There's no doubt in my mind about who took them and why.

As soon as we can, we check on Ezra in his room. He's devastated and scared for both his sister and his mom. I only let Lucas inside the room with him. They were playing video games last time I checked, but it's a poor distraction for everything that's going on..

I have Matt watching the house. I don't want anyone to take him too.

Ryder, Cash, Zay, and Bryson busted inside the door looking for Ava as soon as the guards left. I asked them how they knew something happened since the council's tac team is silent. They said because they were woken up by a feeling of panic, they knew something had happened to Ava. I'm not sure if that's true or not, but that's their story and they're sticking to it.

I sent them home two hours ago. I told them they needed to get some rest. I glance at my brothers, who look just as exhausted as I feel, but there's no way we'll rest. I bet money that Ryder, Cash, Zay, and Bryson never made it home to rest either. They're probably outside keeping their distance, staring at the house, and waiting for our next move.

A knock on the door startles me from my thoughts. None of us make the effort to get up to see who's on the other side. If it's a threat, they probably wouldn't have been knocking anyhow. The council tac team left a long time ago, and they may come back to kill us, but not today. Their job here is done for now. My stomach revolts. I can't believe I used to work for them.

Footsteps approach. "Gentlemen." Our heads snap up to see Silas standing there looking very suspicious.

Az is the first one to get up and get in his face. "Where

the fuck is she?" Az's voice is broken, but he manages to sound menacing, nonetheless.

"Give me one good reason why I shouldn't tear your head off?" Ash says, getting closer to Silas but still keeping a distance.

"Because I know where she is." We collectively growl at his response.

"I know we can't kill a council member, but as of now, I don't give a fuck about the council coming after me. Let them all come," Benji says as I stand from the couch and give our intruder my full attention.

Silas laughs, which makes Benji angrier. "How about I give you something, Benji, something to show that I'm not here to harm any of you," he says with open arms, trying to look non-threatening.

Before we can comprehend his words, he shouts, "Come on in."

We stare at the entryway and—

"Zoe," Benji stutters in disbelief. "Is it really you?" she walks in looking around the house before her eyes land on her brother.

"Hey big brother." Benji moves past me and Silas and grabs his sister, hugging her tightly.

"Why?" Benji asks in a broken and hollow voice.

"She deserves to live her life. I didn't know that the place existed until very recently. Tyler needed the location of the woman, and so I gave it to him knowing you'd free those kids." I really don't know Silas's angle, but he can't be trusted. Silas always has his own agenda. I just don't know what it is. When we don't respond, he continues. "I didn't take her." When the four of us glare at him he says, "I promise." You never know what you're going to get with Silas.

"Where is she?" Az asks, still staring at Zoe like she's going to go crazy and kill us all. Benji notices and scowls at Az. When this is over, we need to all sit down and have a long conversation with Zoe.

"You remember the night Kat killed Krissy?" We nod our heads. "There was smoke that came out of Krissy along with her powers looking for a host."

"Where are you going with this, Silas?" I ask in confusion. I'm trying to figure out if any of his bullshit will help us find Kat.

"Well, Krissy's power was looking for a host, and as I suspected, it latched onto Ava." I gasp. Fuck! "Not only that, but the black shadow that came out of Krissy, well that's a shadow that belongs to the other side."

"Stop fucking with us, Silas," Az growls. "If you're not going to tell us where Kat is then fucking leave before I decide to bleed you to death."

"Hang on, Az. Listen to my story first. That shadow belongs to the portal where the werewolves were locked up. Theo is making Kat open the portal, which means more shadows will come out."

"What was the black smoke?" I ask, remembering it came out of nowhere. I've never seen anything like it before. I don't know what it is, but I have a feeling it's nothing good.

"Death," Silas replies.

CHAPTER 31

ASH

I tense at Silas's words. The thought of the black smoke and how it distorted our vision worries me. I remember switching to my wolf vision and still couldn't see anything in front of me.

"The black smoke was a fail-safe for Theo. If Krissy was dying, she was to release that power. That power was attached to Theo. It came out when the portal opened. I think," he says hesitantly. "It has a mind of its own, but I'm not too sure." He turns away from us briefly before his eyes land on me. I can't tell if he's lying. "Krissy had that shadow locked in place. I told her to do it to have leverage against Theo. Now the shadow is back and has merged with Theo. They've become unstoppable now that the foreign object is attached to him. They both have a goal, and that's to open the portal to their world. That's why we need to make sure Kat doesn't open the portal and let more of those shadow things come to this world. I've seen what that small black smoke can do, and I don't want to see what will happen if a big wave shows up."

I'm trying to wrap my head around all the information Silas is giving us.

"Theo was angry that I found Smart Technologies," Silas continues. "And even more furious I gave you guys the location of his facility. As revenge, he found one of my homes which happened to be the one with the book, the only book that belonged to the violet voyagers also known as Kat's kind. This means she can open the portal if she reads the spell that only her kind can say out loud. Theo spent centuries looking for it, but I kept it hidden. I never thought he'd find my place. If I knew he'd use children to harvest the power he needed to create the portal, I would've stopped it immediately."

"Why are you giving us all this information?" Az asks, holding tightly to his knife. I think Az is planning on throwing it as Silas, but it won't come near him. Silas is too quick.

"Isn't it obvious?" He looks at each of us. "I don't want those black shadows in this world." This is the first time I've ever seen fear in his eyes, but it's gone quickly.

"What do y'all think?" I ask my brothers through our mind link.

"I think this is all fucking crazy, but I don't think he's lying about this," Benji says.

"He's not lying, but I know Silas has his own agenda. What it is, I have no fucking clue," Tyler replies clenching and unclenching his fists.

"Fuck. I can't kill him because I believe him." Az keeps his eyes on Silas, but Silas isn't threatened by any of us.

"I think he does have his own agenda but, as of now, I can't seem to care because we need him to find Kat and Ava," I relay my thoughts to them.

"If you guys are done communicating, let's get the fuck out of here and find your mate and your daughter," Silas says with urgency. He came in here as if he had all the time in the world, but he's just as worried as the rest of us.

Silas looks up at the stairs, and I follow his line of sight but find nothing. This guy is fucking weird, but the man knows too much about things he shouldn't. Maybe one day I'll hold him with my claws and see if he'll spill his secrets. I doubt he'll let me get that close to him, but it's worth a try.

Tyler grabs his phone from his pocket, talking to a beta. Within minutes we hear a van pulling up.

"Zoe, let me show you to your room," Benji tells his sister, guiding her up the stairs.

We watch them leave, and my shoulders relax when he takes her to the third floor. I look at Az and Tyler, and they seem just as relieved as I do.

"Tyler—" I start.

"Already messaged Carter," Tyler answers, his fingers tapping rapidly at his phone. I want someone to keep guard. I don't trust her yet.

When we hear the bedroom door close, we each sprint to our rooms to grab our tac gear. Benji and I make it back to the bottom at the same time, and Az is already down here with Tyler.

Silas sits waiting on the couch, eyes glued to his phone screen. At our rushed appearance, he pockets his phone and stands smoothly.

"Let's go," Silas says, already striding for the front door. We scramble to follow behind him.

Outside, Andrew holds the back door of the idling SUV open for us. Once we're settled in our seats, he slams it shut and hops into the driver's side as Carter takes shotgun. The engine revs, and we peel away.

Our betas got our guards together and are following behind us in a caravan of vehicles.

After two hours trekking through the forest, we finally stop. None of us talked the whole way. I glance over at Silas. He looks relaxed, but there is a tightness in the corner of his eyes.

He says he wants to help, and maybe he does, but I know there's something more going on with this. He's got his own reasons, and he isn't sharing any of them.

Once we get out of the van, there are ATVs waiting for us. I thought this was it, I thought we were here. I didn't think we had to travel more. I don't let the disappointment show. I'm anxious to see my mate to make sure she's unharmed. If they've hurt Ava or Katarina in any way, they're going to regret what they've done. We will destroy each and every single person there.

"Get on," Silas says.

My brothers and I take one of the ATVs, and Silas and Andrew take the other. Az takes the driver's seat, and I take the back with Benji. I hear Tyler and Az bickering, but I pay them no mind. They'll take care of their own shit. Eventually Az moves and Tyler gets in the driver's seat.

"Have the others shift into wolves and follow us." They don't need to be told twice. They shed their clothes and shift.

The air gets thicker the longer we drive, and my nerves get the best of me. I haven't had this feeling since I was a kid. I try to contain my emotions before I accidentally shift and the beast takes over, destroying everything in its path. As it is, he's pacing back and forth in my head.

I look over at Benji, knowing he has a lot on his mind with his sister showing up, but I need to know I can trust him to be here with us.

"My mind is focused, Ash," he says angrily through our mind link. His eyes shift to mine, and I only nod once.

Silas's ATV finally stops, and Tyler pulls up alongside him.

"Katarina." I can finally sense her, but she isn't answering. *"Katarina,"* I say again, this time more anxiously. I don't have a good feeling. If your mind connection is open again, this means—Oh no.

The ground shakes violently. My brothers and I look at each other with wide eyes.

"We're too late," Silas says, that's when a thick black fog surrounds us.

Ava has all of Krissy's magic. I look at my daughter in shock, but her eyes are cast down.

"This worked out better than I hoped," Theo says with glee.

"Your daughter has Krissy's magic? But how? When did she die? And why weren't we made aware of this?" one of the human-looking supernaturals asks. He has a long black tail that swings back and forth, but he could easily pass for human.

"Well Darragh," Theo begins dramatically. "Kat here killed her days ago." There's a collective gasp among the members.

"Even more reason to terminate Kat now. If she's able to kill someone as powerful as Krissy then we should get rid of her. She's a threat to us." The angel's shapely white curls are crowned by a halo that casts a soft glow across her ageless features. Despite her beauty, her full lips are pursed in disdain. Her delicate brows arch over her eyes with a narrowed contempt. She holds her flowing wings arched up in a gesture of authority. The feathers rustle with glittering white crystals as she speaks.

Ava looks at me fearfully as the guards take slow, pointed steps toward me, and it breaks my heart that I can't reassure her. I want to tell her that we'll both be okay. I still have The Kiss of Death strapped to my leg beneath my nightgown. We have a chance to survive this, but I stay silent, begging her with my eyes to trust me.

As the two guards get closer, I hunker down, reaching beneath my skirt to feel for my weapon, but before I can rip the blade free from its holder, a shadow steps right in front of me and swallows the guards whole, leaving nothing behind.

Everyone gasps, including myself, and I stumble back to get away from it.

Theo opens his arms wide and smirks as the shadows wrap around his body. The council members clamor to their feet, stumbling over each other and knocking their seats over in the rush to save themselves.

"Oh, don't be scared now. I haven't shown you all who I truly am." Theo's eyes begin to glow, and a deep shade of red bleeds into the whites until there's nothing left of his familiar dark stare.

"How is this possible?" the same female angel asks.

"Our ancestors got rid of you all ages ago." The male angel eyes Theo with hesitance.

"Well, Evelyn, Oliver, to answer your questions, they got rid of all of the lycans except for me." Theo revels in their surprise.

Evelyn's beautiful face distorts in horror as she stumbles farther from Theo. She points a finger at him before turning it on me and then Ava. "Kill that whole family," she shouts. There are forty of the council's guards that come running, ready to attack.

Theo doesn't do anything, just stands there with a smile on his face as they run toward him.

The shadow unfurls from his body like a great black demon stretching thousands of wispy arms toward the men and women of the council. No one notices me when I start to move toward Ava. This isn't our fight. She shouldn't be here to see her father this way, but she is, and I can't shield her from the horrific scene unfolding before her wide eyes.

I grab her hand and pull her toward me.

"Mom..."

"Yeah, I see it too," I say as we watch the black smoke consume all of them one by one, leaving nothing behind but their dying screams that are carried away on the wind.

What the fuck is that?

Theo turns toward us next, his red eyes settling on our daughter. "Now Ava, dear, come here please." I hold onto Ava even tighter, knowing that I'll probably leave bruises on her skin, but I don't dare loosen my grip. I don't want her anywhere near Theo.

"No," I respond, surprised that my voice isn't as shaky as I feel. "She's not going anywhere near you."

I have to kill him. I wish I had my wolf with me right now. I need her.

You are your wolf, a small voice says. I don't know where that bravery came from, but I hold onto it tightly.

Ava shakes in my arms uncontrollably, and when I try to tighten my grip, she pushes me back with an unnatural strength. She stumbles to her knees, eyes closed and face pinched in pain.

"Ava, what's wrong, what's happening?" She throws her head back and looks slowly toward the sky, then turns to me with a frantic expression. Her eyes are as bright red as Theo's. Her body is changing, growing, and her clothing pulls apart at the seams. I let go of her arm and watch, knowing there's nothing I can do to help my little girl.

Every piece of clothing she was wearing earlier is on the floor in shreds. I look up as she towers over me at six feet tall.

"You did it," Theo says proudly.

I take a step back trying to get a better look. Just a couple days ago we talked about how lycans no longer exist and now my daughter is one.

"Don't be scared." Theo's voice sounds foreign to my ears, when I look back at him, I see he's turned too.

Wolves can't talk but lycans can? He stands on two legs while the smoke surrounds him.

I try to shift into my wolf but still can't. At least I still have my weapon with me.

Theo walks closer with long strides, and I blindly retreat, one slow step at a time until my back hits the side of a tree. His long legs and giant body loom over me, and I look back quickly to see that I've hit a dead end.

When I try to run the other way, Theo is there right in front of me with the shadow hovering behind him. My eyes drift behind him quickly trying to gauge what the fuck that void is, but I have no clue. I've never seen anything like this before.

"This shadow was born on the other side of the locked portal where my people are trapped." Theo answers me like he knew what I was thinking.

"Theo, I had nothing to do with—"

"Of course you didn't, but you're going to be the one to help me open the portal."

Nope, not happening.

"How? I just learned the use of my power." I try to reach the bottom of my dress and slowly start pulling it up, but when he notices, I act like I have an itch and let the gown fall.

"Not to worry."

I don't like the sound of that, I should probably start panicking.

"This book is going to help you open it." He opens his paw—er claws, and the black shadow hovers over it and drops a book in his hand.

He offers me the book, and I take it with shaking hands. The book's cover is violet and the pages are a lighter shade. It isn't thick at all, maybe only about twenty pages. I try to read the script, but I have no clue what the words say.

I flip through the pages and stop at a particular one that has the image of a very familiar blade running across a person's neck.

"That's the one we need." My heart stops in fear, nearly dropping the book.

I look back at him again. "You need a sacrifice to open and close the portal?"

I look over at the only two council members left, and I notice that the hunters holding them down are the same men we thought had been killed. They were working for Theo all along.

Wanting to stall for a chance to grab my weapon, I ask, "What's the difference between a witch and me? Why couldn't Krissy open this?"

"This portal is unlike any other world. It's been closed off even before I was born. This portal houses a different breed of supernaturals." He smiles coyly before going on. "You know who else lives on the other side of this portal, Kat?" I swallow through a thick lump in my throat. I already know the answer to his question, but he voices it out loud anyway. "Your kind, the violet voyagers. The first time the portal opened was in Nicaragua, that's why there were so many of your kind living there. The ones that managed to escape to the other side made this place their home."

Theo turns his attention to the black shadow as if he's speaking with it, and I know this is my only chance to make a move while he's distracted.

I drop the book on the floor and reach beneath my gown for my weapon. As the black shadow has temporarily taken on a solid form, I run toward it with my fist clenching The Kiss of Death tightly.

Before Theo can react, I stab the black shadow with my weapon. The shadow turns misty again, swallowing my weapon whole. I try calling for it in my mind the way I did the night I killed Krissy, but nothing happens.

What the fuck? My mouth hangs open in surprise, what the hell do I do now?

"My patience is running thin, Kat," Theo growls, and I'd be lying if I said I wasn't afraid. "Read the book, now!" he roars, and I can feel the ground vibrate as he spits out those words.

He shoves the book at me again.

"I won't do it, Theo. I won't open it. I was chosen to guard the portal and keep it closed, and that's exactly what I'm going to do." I stand my ground. I'm not letting him bully me again, not anymore. I'm not the same woman cowering at the kitchen table under his judgmental stare. I'm a fucking warrior.

Theo looks at the shadow and nods toward Ava, and my entire stomach flips in pure panic as it immediately pursues our daughter. Images of the council members disappearing into the smoke bring a sharp cry from the back of my throat. "Theo, No!"

"I can make it so you'll never see Ava again," he taunts.

What choice do I have? This is the only way he can get me to open the portal and he knows it. I'd do anything for my kids.

He shoves Aisling toward me, she crouches on the floor with fear in her eyes and tape over her mouth. She's being held down by two people so she can't move. Just earlier she was looking at me like dirt and now her eyes are filled with terror.

I look at the last two members of the council rooted in

place by Theo's dark magic, and they struggle against their invisible binds, unable to speak or scream. They will die tonight just as the others did, of that I'm sure.

Theo hands me a blade and shoves the woman to her knees in front of me. "I'm sorry," I whisper as tears stream down my face. It's an impossible decision, but I won't risk my daughter's life.

I do as I saw in the picture. With one swipe, blood gushes from the wound in her throat, and her mouth opens and closes in shock. Theo quickly takes the knife, replacing it with the book.

"Form a circle around Kat with the blood," he directs, and the hunters do as he says.

There's no time to freak out. I look down at the book, and the words are foreign to my eyes, but as I read, there's something so familiar about them that it almost scares me. Theo is onto something about this book belonging to my people.

A hole appears out of thin air, growing bigger and bigger the closer I get to the end of the passage. Once my words stop, a thick cloud of darkness settles around me like smoke. I drop the book, there's screaming and shouting, and I realize it's coming from me.

"Ava! Ava!" I shout, but the shadows are too thick to see anything, just like the night Krissy died.

A stampede of . . . something is coming out of the hole. I can't see what it is, but I know it's nothing good.

"*Katarina,*" Ash yells through our mind link. "*Katari-na,*" he shouts again, but my mind is too occupied trying to get to my daughter.

The wind is blowing harder and faster. The ground underneath me rumbles as foreign steps jump out of the portal.

"Ava!" I keep yelling, but I can't move. I crouch down looking for the book I dropped. I'm not sure how I'll be able to read the spell to open the portal, but I'll have to try. I get on my knees, hoping and praying that whatever hoard is coming out of the void doesn't step on me.

It's slow moving since the wind passing by me is so harsh. I crawl in the direction I think I've dropped it. I feel like Velma when she drops her glasses and is too blind to find them.

A minute later, my hand touches the book, I try to pick it up but can't. I feel around only to find someone's foot on top of the book, keeping me from picking it up. I look up and can only see red eyes. I stifle my scream. I don't know if it's Theo or another lycan.

It picks me up from my throat, and my feet no longer touch the ground. I try to kick the body, but the lycan's arms are too long for me to do much damage.

"You're not closing the portal, Kat," Theo growls. How the hell can he see through the darkness surrounding us? "Not until every last lycan is back where they belong."

"Theo," a gravelly voice sounds from behind him. I flick my eyes toward the voice only to see red eyes. "It's good to be back."

"Beau, it's nice to have you back. I need you to take some of the lycans down there." His body moves slightly, and I think Theo is pointing in the direction he wants them to go. "I have no doubt her mates are coming back for her and Ava. They're wolves, you can kill them all."

"Finally, payback," Beau grumbles and leaves me alone with Theo once again.

"We're getting our revenge, Kat. We're going to kill every last one of your kind," Theo says, squeezing just a little bit tighter before we're both knocked over.

Theo snarls, "Ava!"

"I can't let that happen, Dad. I'm fated to four wolves."

"Impossible," he snaps back with a long howl. "Our nature won't allow wolves and lycans to be together."

"It's true, Dad, and I can't let you kill them." I can't even process the words Ava said, but I tuck them away for a later discussion with my wolf.

Speaking of my wolf. With the tranquilizer gone from my system and my powers pulsing through me, why hasn't she come out?

"Oh I've been out. I'm just trying to figure out how the hell we're going to close the fucking portal," she responds.

I scramble wildly along the ground to find the fallen book.

"Here you go, Mom." Ava shoves the book into my hands. "I'll tell you the words and you can repeat them."

"Ava no! If you speak those words, you'll die. Why do you think Krissy never did it? You don't have my power. Those words will destroy you." I can't let that happen.

"So how the hell are you supposed to close it if I can't say the words and you can't see them?"

Theo crackles. "The only way to close the portal is from the other side."

My heart drops.

"How many shadows have come out?" Theo asks someone.

"Five."

One is too many. I don't want to think about what five would do.

"I don't think we should let that many out. We won't be able to control them."

"My daughter can," Theo replies.

Theo goes down with a loud grunt. "Ava can you see?" Az asks as he fights Theo. I can't see anything, but I can hear all the grunts the men are making.

My heart flutters in happiness, but the feeling is short-lived when I think of my mates being among the shadows that could easily swallow them whole.

"I can see," Ava responds.

"Leave this place," Az says with a loud snarl.

Ava grabs my hand and we take hurried steps away from my mate. I pull back, and her red eyes turn to me, standing out like two smoldering embers in the endless dark.

"Ava, I need you to find Julian or Detra," I tell her.

"Why?" she asks. Because they're going to be the ones I sacrifice to close the portal I think to myself.

"Just do it." She disappears, and I really wish I could see what the hell is going on. I can't see my mates, but I know they're close.

Moments later, heavy footsteps grow closer. "I found Julian," my daughter says. "But he looks to be dying."

Perfect, shit, well not perfect for him, but for me it means less struggling.

"Take Julian and me to the other side of the portal." I can't leave like Az wanted me to. I have to close it.

"But Mom—"

"Ava, do it now!" I yell. I may not have another chance now that Theo is distracted. There's no way I'm letting more of those shadow things come out.

She grabs my elbow, and her hand is scaly and hairy, so different from a wolf, but she's my daughter, and I will never treat her any differently. I grab Julian by his collar, dragging him with me.

I stumble over something on the ground, but Ava is quick to pick me up. We walk again until I'm pushed on my back by a snarling lycan snapping his jaw at me.

I'm done being afraid. I grab the open jaw dropping Julian and using both hands, placing one hand on the upper mouth and placing the other on the bottom, stretching it. It tries to move back and forth, but I have a tight grip on it.

I need to end the lycans life now before it's too late. I'm no longer afraid. I'll do what I have to do to survive. The bone cracks and the howling stops. I throw the dead weight off to the side.

I frantically try to look for Ava, but it's pitch black, and even with my wolf eyes, I can't see anything. What the fuck am I going to do? How the hell am I going to find her?

"Rely on our senses," my wolf reminds me.

I take a moment to breathe and catch her sweet peach scent in the air. I run toward her as she yelps. I pick up the lycan that hurt my daughter and extend my claws. I listen for a heartbeat, and that's when my hand strikes, pushing into flesh and pulling out the heart.

"Ava!" I shout. "Are you okay?"

"My head is pounding, but I'm okay for now." I let out a long breath.

"Come on, Mom." She takes my hand in hers, leading me to Julian's body, and we start walking again. Without my sight, the task before me feels impossible, but the lycan's uneven footsteps and the sharp pull of their claws grabbing at my flesh gives me direction in this battle. The killing becomes a lot easier when you don't think about taking a life. Not sure if that's a good thing or a bad thing, but for now, it's helping me survive.

I hate not knowing if my guys are fine, but there's no time to check in on them, I just have to hope they're holding on.

I know when we make it to the portal because it's calling to me, wanting me to go to the other side.

I turn to look at my daughter's red eyes, "Ava—"

"Mom, please don't do it," she sobs.

"I have to, Ava," I say, gripping the book tightly.

"There has to be another way."

"There isn't, I'm it." I put the book underneath my armpit, squeezing it tightly so it won't fall. Searching for her hands, I hold onto them tightly. "Ava, I love you and your brother so much. Please tell my mates that they've made me love life again, and I will never forget any of them. They will always have my heart."

"Mom, please," she begs.

"I have to go. And you have to get out of here. After this is over, I don't want your father capturing you." Without another word, I drop her hands and run to the other side of the void, landing on both feet.

As soon as I emerge on the side of the void, the suffocating black smoke dissipates. The darkness plaguing my vision evaporates, sight fully returning now that I'm through the portal.

I look around this familiar yet alien place. It's a wasteland, with gray dirt and crumbling stone ruins. Creatures and lycans stampede past me trying to reach the portal.

With my vision cleared of the shadow, I can finally see the full chaos and desperation. The revealed carnage is almost too much, but at least the return of my senses lets me fully take in the situation.

"We have to do it now!" The urgency in my wolf's voice startles me.

I scramble through the book, looking for the familiar page Theo gave me. I extend my claws and slice Julian's neck, spreading the blood as I saw the hunters doing and soon after I start reading the words.

My head pounds as the guys try to communicate with me. I know my mates have a feeling I'm about to do something dangerous.

As I say the words, black shadows swarm around me. They're blowing harder and faster than the air on the other side.

The shadows laugh at my distress. "We ate your kind.

That's when the violet voyagers found the new world and made it their home. Only a handful survived and made it to the other side, but it looks like they're nearly all dead," the shadow says as it gets closer to me.

"Kat!" Fucking Ryder! What the hell is he doing here? "We're coming to help you," he shouts.

Oh no! I tilt my head up, smelling the air. They're all here.

There is fighting on the other side of the black shadows. I watch with wide eyes as the shadows take a more solid form. There are three of them and five of us. Two of them fight the figures except Cash, who's taking on one of them by himself.

Cash glances at me. "Just read it, Kat!" he shouts as he struggles with the shadow.

As I recite the last of the words, I watch as the portal begins to close. The black shadow has backed up momentarily as if shocked that it's closing.

I use that opportunity to shout "Run!" As I start running toward the portal. My body thrums knowing that if I miss the portal, I'll be stuck here forever. I get knocked down and the book flies. There's no time for me to grab it, I pick myself up and continue to sprint.

Their footsteps are right behind me.

"We're almost there!" I yell out. "We're going to make it to the other side."

I don't stop no matter how exhausted my body is. Finally, I jump and make it to the other side of the portal, landing on the ground.

I look behind me, and just as the four of them extend their legs, they're engulfed by the black shadows and the portal closes, leaving Ryder, Bryson, Zay, and Cash on the other side with no way of opening the portal back up.

Az

Everything is silent besides Ava's cries and screams. The shadows have lifted, and we can finally see the gore, limbs, and the blood staining the forest.

The lycans watch us warily and with so much loathing. They want to destroy us, even if we're not the ones who locked them on the other side of the portal.

The lycans are ruthless fucking beasts, but so are we. They're not built like us, and we're not built like them. It took our guys two to one to fight them. They had the advantage of being able to see us when we couldn't see them, but they lost more than we did. I just hope Theo was among the dead lycans. I almost had him but he ran away from me.

My pack stands on the opposite side. How we manage to get on opposite sides before the darkness lifted is beyond me, but I'm glad we are because my focus is on Ava and Kat and not on fighting. As much as I like blood, I need to make sure my mate and Ava are okay.

Kat is in the center of the clearing between the lycans and the wolves. She's crouched on the floor, staring in horror as the portal closes, leaving the kids on the other side.

I'm too stunned to move. This hasn't happened to me in a very long time. Usually I'd be focused on bloodshed, but nearly losing my mate and losing the kids has diverted my attention to making sure my family's well-being is okay.

Wait, where the fuck did Silas go?

Ava tries to claw her way from Ash's grip, but he won't let her go. He's holding her waist tightly. She's still in lycan form and very strong. Ash tries to whisper in her ear, but she's having none of it.

If those four are really her mates, which I believe they are, her heart has just shattered into a million pieces. I don't know if she'll ever be able to recover from the loss of her mates. I know I couldn't live without Kat; she's my whole world.

Kat gets up from the ground with tears running down her flushed cheeks. She looks around at both sides until she spots her daughter. That's when the lycans start to back away.

We let them leave for now.

"No!" Ava screams as Ash guides her into her mother's arms. She's trying to push Kat away, so Kat holds on to her tighter. She still manages to get out of her mom's grip, but Benji grabs her before she runs off.

Ava pounds against him, kicking and screaming until she finally sags against him crying. My heart breaks for her. The threat is gone but not without consequences.

Ava will never be the same after this.

"Open it, Mom!" she wails. Her pain is raw.

"I can't, Ava, I'm so sorry." Kat goes down on her knees with her head hung low. I'm immediately there by her side, trying to get her to stand up. She leans against me, and I hold onto her. "The book is on the other side, and the spell was so complex, I don't remember it. I would've happily sacrificed someone, but the problem is the spell, I don't—" she sighs heavily, "I don't remember."

The lycans have disappeared. My enhanced vision picks up subtle movements in the shadows. The lycans haven't fled. The five inky black shadows still swirling around us must be their doing, concealing them from view.

"No . . . no this can't be happening," Ava chants over and over again in pain and defeat.

"Theo, show yourself!" Kat screams as she looks around the forest.

There's nothing.

"Theo!" Kat calls out angrier this time.

"Love," Ash whispers in her ear gently. "I think he's gone. Disappeared with the rest of them. We'll find him, I promise you."

Kat laughs, there's a hollow sound to it that I don't like.

"No, he's still here," she replies, scanning the trees with her violet eyes.

"Everyone is gone but us." Tyler is now in front of Kat while Ash is on the opposite side of me.

Her shoulders are tense. I move my fingers, massaging her, hopefully getting her to relax a bit. She reaches back, putting her hands in my pockets before pulling them out and walking off. I drop my hands, missing the feel of my mate.

She looks down at the floor as if she can spot his distinct footprints. She can't though, there are too many. Still, she looks down and follows them out into the heavy forest leaving the clearing.

"We should get going," I say gently, following behind her.

"No. Not until I kill Theo." She looks at Benji, still holding Ava. "Have someone take her home." Benji nods. Then her words are barely a whisper. "I don't want her to see me kill her father."

How I wished at this moment it was Theo stuck on the other side instead of Ryder, Bryson, Zay, and Cash. My brothers and I will never forgive ourselves for not protecting them. I look over at Ava. I don't think she'll ever forgive us either.

All the guards along with Andrew and Carter leave us, taking Ava with them. It's now only my brothers, Kat and Joseph.

"Kat," Tyler tries again, but she silences him with one look and he backs away reluctantly to give her space. After thirty minutes, we continue to stand in the middle of this carnage, our group long gone.

"Come out, Theo." Her voice is exhausted, but she's so sure that he's hiding. My senses don't tell me he's here, but I won't dare go against my mate. She's been through a lot today.

Three huge lycans come out of the trees. Their red eyes

glare at us and a shadow stands behind them. I quickly run to Kat's side and protect her, but I'm pushed by a strong set of hands and fly into the base of a tree.

I stand up but stumble. I got hit pretty hard and the world won't stop spinning.

I knew he was hiding somewhere. I knew the stupid dark shadows were cloaking him. Theo wouldn't have left without trying to kill us.

He wants us dead.

I'm surrounded. I'm staring at the three in front of me, but my eyes are solely focused on Theo in the middle.

We're a threat to him, it's why I sent Ava back home. She's had enough suffering to last a lifetime. I don't want her to see Theo and me destroying each other.

My heart grieves for my daughter. I don't think she'll ever forgive me for leaving her guys on the other side. I'll never forgive myself as I remember the look of horror in each of their faces right before they were swept away by the shadows.

I hate that I'll have to bring the terrible news to the kids' parents, tell them I've failed my first assignment as Luna. The thought of speaking to their parents and delivering the devastating news makes me nauseous. All I can think about now is that they won't graduate high school or go to college. I should've been more assertive, I should've used my power of persuasion to get them to leave, but I didn't, and now they're gone.

I push my thoughts away for the moment, staying focused on my target instead. Only one of us is making it out alive after tonight. The dead bodies that were lying on the ground have been absorbed by one of the shadows.

A savage snarling erupts behind me, the high-pitched sounds of lycans tearing into my guys. My men shriek of fury and pain, along with the sickening rip of flesh. The tang of fresh blood floods the air.

My muscles scream to whirl around, to protect my mates. But the lycan's eyes blaze before me, his hulking form ready to strike. This is his strategy, he wants me distracted.

I hear bodies slam to the ground and the struggles of my guys trying to get back up, but I know my guys won't go down that easily.

"Kat. How'd you know I was waiting?" Theo asks, his voice rough, still in his lycan form as the three men join his side once again.

Behind me, I hear the labored breathing and pained groans of my mates as they struggle to rise. I let out a small breath of relief. They spit curses through bared teeth.

The lycans have shred their bodies viciously, but the wounds are not fatal. Now my men seethe with vengeance, raging auras pulsing around their large forms as they ready themselves to rejoin this vicious fight. My mates are by my side, bloodied but unbroken.

"Because I didn't keep the portal open long enough for the other lycans to get out, so now you want to kill me for it," I reply. He spent years searching for someone like me and then spent more time trying to figure out how to open the portal. I've ruined his plans, and now that he has no use for me, he wants to take my life. "But I'm going to kill you instead."

"There's no way you can kill me, Kat. Your powers are useless against me. Your only hope was The Kiss of Death, and now that's gone." The shadow looms behind him ready to strike on Theo's command.

I hate this man, and I will never get back the years I wasted with him. I want to be the better person and let him live, but as long as he's alive, he's a threat to my kids, and he won't stop until he finds a way to kill me.

I need to end this now.

"Shred her to pieces," Theo says as the two lycans run toward me.

At his command, two huge lycans sprint toward me, jaws gaping and claws outstretched. Moonlight glints off their jagged talons, now slick with fresh blood.

Time seems to slow. I brace myself, ready to meet their frenzied attacks head on. But before the beasts reach me, two forms collide with them from the side.

Ash, battered but unyielding, tackles one lycan in a blur. His fangs sink into a furry neck even as the lycan's claws rake viciously across his back, opening savage gashes.

As the four of them fight viciously, more massive forms materialize from the darkness. A pack of four more lycans now prowl at the edges of the clearing.

The other lycan is intercepted by Joseph's crushing charge. They slam to the ground in a frenzy of snapping teeth. Joseph's arms swing again and again, black blood flying through the air with each savage chop.

After a few breathless moments, the lycan's struggle grows weak, then it ceases altogether as Joseph's relentless blows overwhelm it.

Ash's fangs sink deeper into his opponent's furry neck until, with a sickening crunch, the beast goes limp in his jaws, and both lycans lie unmoving in spreading pools of blood.

My gaze briefly lands on my mates fighting in human form trying to kill the four other lycans apart from the two that were standing next to him.

"Now it's our chance to kill him," my wolf says viciously.

Theo grabs me by my hair and throws me. Ouch! Fuck, that hurt. I land on my stomach, and before I can get up, he's on me, fisting my hair and holding me in place. At this rate, he's going to leave me bald.

This time, he pulls my body from the ground and throws me against a tree. I slide down on my butt, knowing it's going to be bruised no matter how fast I heal.

I debate whether to shift into a wolf, but there's no time to make a decision because he comes for me, but this time I'm prepared and ball my hand into a fist that connects with his nose. I hear a loud crack, but I don't stop there. I hit him as though he's the punching bag I use at the gym.

His face is a bloodied mess, but I still don't stop releasing all of my aggression and anger. Even if I wanted to stop, I don't think I could. My body is in a trance, and it only has one goal in mind, and that's to end Theo's life for good.

All the pain he's put me through, all the shame, all the embarrassment. I will never again feel this way.

The black shadow looms over me, distorting my vision. I get off of Theo trying to fight it off.

"Stand back and go with the others. I should be done here soon," Theo says as he grabs my neck. "She's mine."

The black shadow dissipates, and I see Theo's angry red eyes, bloody nose, and his body that's about to swell up.

I know my guys are still trying to fight the lycans, but it's not like I can yell out and ask for help.

He's cutting off my air supply, making it harder to breathe. I start to get light headed, but I still have one more thing up my sleeve.

He's too focused on my face to notice what I'm doing with the rest of my body. I feel for Az's knife, the one I took from him earlier. I hope he's not looking for it, and I hope he doesn't need it.

I find the hilt of the knife, and before I can plan this further, I shove it in his eye the same way I did with Dan the first night I was turned into a wolf. But this time, I'm not running away—not anymore. I'm going to see this through.

He stumbles loudly with a screeching growl that has my body shivering at the tone.

"You'll pay for this, Kat," he says, still not letting me go.

His claws puncture holes on the side of my neck. Everything that's happening feels slow like there's a movie playing right in front of my eyes.

I'm going to die, I think to myself. The least I can do is bring him down with me.

My body begins to tremble with the last bit of adrenaline I have left. Before he can pull Az's knife out of his eye, I grab it and stab the other one. He lets me go, gripping his eyes with both hands, stumbling through the forest and growling loudly. I just hope that the shadow doesn't come back. I have no energy to stand on two legs, when he lets me go, I fall hard on the ground again.

"You fucking bitch!" he yells out, but it sounds so far away.

My claws come out, and I drag my heavy body to his. I'm trying to keep up with him as he edges backward. I need to crawl faster to get to him, but my body is giving out.

He stumbles over a tree stump, and this is my chance to end him, but now I just want to lay here and never get up.

A pool of blood surrounds me, and I can't tell if it's his or mine. I'm starting to see black spots.

"Six more feet," I chant to try and motivate myself to keep going; that's all I need to get to him. With the little strength I can muster, I hold onto Az's blade and continue to crawl to him.

I kneel next to him. "Goodbye Theo," I say as I stab the blade into his chest over and over until everything turns black.

I wake up with my body draped over a man's lap, the smell of lavender and leather wrapping around me like a familiar, warm blanket. My body aches all over, and when I open my eyes, the ground rushes beneath us, dirt clouding around my face and making me cough. I whimper as we hit something on the ground, whoever is driving the ATV is slamming hard on the pedal.

Az growls something unintelligible, or maybe it just sounds that way to me. Amara's soft voice is next to me. When did she show up? She's sitting next to Az.

"We don't know how long the spell will keep the shadows at bay, it's best if we get the fuck outta here before it breaks." Amara's voice quivers in fear.

The next thing I know, I'm waking up in my bed.

My body is sore. "You're awake!" I look over at Benji with relief in his eyes. He's leaning against my dresser.

"Wh—What happened?" I ask, my voice rough. "And what day is it?"

"You lost a lot of fucking blood, Kat," Az says as he walks into the room. "We almost lost you." I'm actually surprised to be alive. I didn't think I'd make it. "We only just got here three hours ago."

"Where's Ava and Ezra?" I ask instead, trying to forget everything that's happened to me.

"They're in their rooms waiting for you," Tyler says, standing by the door and assessing my injuries, which I'm sure he already did when I passed out.

"And—" I'm almost afraid to speak his name aloud because I'm afraid if I do, it'll somehow summon him.

"He's dead," Az says as he sits on the right side of my bed. My body relaxes as tears begin to fall freely.

I'm joyous but also exhausted. I shift uncomfortably on my bed, wondering what my kids are going to think.

"It'll be about a week until you're fully recovered. Your body is spent and needs to rest," Ash says as he sits on the other side of my bed.

"Did I—" I can't bring myself to say it aloud, but he knows what I'm asking. Did I kill their dad?

"Yeah," Az replies, grabbing my hands and holding onto them tightly.

"Can you have them come here?" I ask, worried about the repercussions of what I've done.

"Kat, you should probably rest," Ash says gently as he runs his fingers through my hair.

"No, I want to talk to them now." My tone is desperate now. I need to see my children.

They share a look before Benji says, "I'll get them." He exits the room, and I sit on the bed trying to calm my nerves.

"Ava is a lycan," I tell them.

"We know," Az says. "She'll always have a place in our pack if she chooses." I knew they'd say that, but my body relaxes with his reassurance.

A minute later, Ava and Ezra walk into the room. I hold my breath, my body filling up with nerves. I don't know what to expect. I don't know if they'll hate me for what I've done to their father.

Az, Ash, Benji, and Tyler back out of the room, leaving us alone. Ezra has dark circles around his eyes like he's barely slept. Ava looks even worse. Her eyes are red like she hasn't slept.

"So . . ." Ezra starts. "Is Dad gone?" My heartbeat thrums wildly inside my chest.

"Yeah . . ." I say, slowly watching their reactions.

"Now I don't have to fear him trying to capture me and taking me with him," Ava says with relief and a tear in her eye.

"And I don't have to worry about him coming back for you, Mom," Ezra says.

"I'm so sorry," I tell them. My head hangs low.

"I know, Mom," Ava replies as she sobs.

"Ava—" I want to apologize, to say something, anything, but she cuts me off.

"Not today, Mom," she says sadly as she walks out of the room.

It's been one month since we lost Ryder, Bryson, Zay, and Cash. My ex-husband is dead, my best friend, Jess, is dead. I've killed so many supernaturals, I don't want to see death anymore. I deserve my happiness along with my mates and kids.

The days following the events have been used for healing. Every time Theo comes to mind, I can't believe he was a lycan and he was always such a threat to me and the kids.

Ezra is coping. He says playing video games helps him deal with the duress he experienced. I also have him in therapy. My kids have been through a lot, and I want them to have a safe place to let their feelings out. Ezra is doing much better and is finally sleeping through the night.

Ava is a different story, she misses her men and avoids anyone who tries to talk to her. She spends most of her time alone. She eats and showers only because I make her. She's a shell of her former self. My mates don't try to convince me she'll be okay because that would be a lie.

We're hoping that she'll survive the loss of her mates, but as of now, it's not looking so good. All I have is hope that it will get easier for her over time.

I found out that my kind has died, and my kids and I are the only ones left, but my kids don't have my powers, so that just leaves me.

As soon as I managed to get out of bed, which was an hour after I woke banged up from the fight, my mates and I went to each of the parents' houses of Ryder, Bryson, Zay, and Cash. It was the hardest thing I've ever had to do, to tell their families that their kids are gone. Their cries, their anguish, their pain was difficult and raw. I mourned right along with them. I told them if they never wanted to see my face that I'd understand, but even though they all forgave me, I don't think I'll ever be able to forgive myself for not bringing them back.

I hope the guys are truly dead because if they aren't, I can't imagine what they'd be going through. I hate that there's no way for me to open the portal back up. The book was left on the other side. I hoped Silas would show up and help me find a way to retrieve it, but he hasn't yet. Silas shows up when he wants to.

My mates have taken the loss of the kids hard too. They were under their care, even if the kids weren't supposed to be there. It was our responsibility to ensure their safety, and we failed.

I know what my powers are and what I am now. I see why Jess had to hide who I was. I was chosen to keep the portal from opening, yet I opened it and let four of those black shadows in along with who knows how many lycans.

There is no way to know what exactly escaped until they decide to show their faces. Whatever else came through will surely bring death, I'm sure of it. It's just a matter of time before they try to take over.

After news spread that the council had been dismantled, we've had alphas from other packs come to show their loyalty to us. I'm as uncomfortable as Az looks when they bend at the knee and swear allegiance to us. I never thought of myself as a leader, but I'm learning what makes a good one from a bad one.

The council wanted to prevent my mates and me from taking control of the shifter community. They believed that if the shifters took control, it would mean they'd lose their right to control their own kind. According to my mates, other supernaturals are fighting for power. We take care of our shifters, and we don't worry about the others. I'm not sure what's going to happen to the other races of supernaturals, nor do I care. I have my family to look after.

Every time I try to talk to Ava, she won't utter more than two words to me. She's always cooped up in her room and only comes out when we make her. She's distanced herself from her friends, from Ezra, from me. I want to ask her more about her powers, but she says she lost them the day she lost her guys. I don't really believe her, but for now, I'll let her keep her secrets.

She trains with my mates as a lycan. My guys say she always shows up on time and she doesn't give them shit. I think she likes their practices because it's an outlet for her pain and aggression.

Amara trains Ava with spells and potions, but so far,

she thinks Ava keeps her powers locked up tightly. One day something may trigger her to lash out and use her powers, but Amara wants to make sure Ava doesn't harm anyone by accident. Amara says she goes through the motions but isn't really present during their study sessions.

Sometimes I find her in the library searching for anything on lycans, but every time I catch her, she quickly closes the book and walks away. Sometimes I want to go out and hunt a lycan and use my power of persuasion on him or her to get them to teach Ava her history, but I know it's a bad idea. If I take one, the whole community will come looking for the one I kidnapped, and that would just lead to another massacre.

There are moments I wake up in a cold sweat, thinking about the other world I belong to and those dark voids. I look back at the day, knowing I couldn't have done anything different, even if I tell myself that I should have found another way. The lycans and the dark shadows have been quietly lying low since I killed Theo.

Amara wards our property to alert us when a different supernatural species crosses our lands. She spends long hours trying to figure out how to kill those black shadows. She hasn't found a way yet. We're all hopeful she can find answers before they decide to attack.

I'm trying to take it day by day, finally able to live in harmony with my mates. They cherish me, and for the first time, I know what it is to be loved. I'm always taken care of and never judged. I can be myself with them and never fear any backlash. I roam our lands freely without worry, for the first time in a long time, I'm happy.

Epilogue

Well, it looks like Ash really did knock me up. Our son Nolan is a year old and is a little daredevil. He likes to run everywhere and get into anything he's not supposed to. I can barely keep up. I never thought I'd have more kids, but I love him just the way I love Ezra and Ava. I'm glad to have more help than what I did the first two times.

When Nolan was born, it brought more life into Ava. Suddenly she was there helping and taking on the big sister role.

He's a miniature version of Ash with platinum hair. My other mates love him just as much as they love my older kids.

Az is so careful and caring. I love to see this nurturing side of him. Benji loves to play the guitar, putting Nolan right to sleep every time.

When Tyler has him, he sets Nolan on his lap, always talking to him about computers. They're all part of him in their own way, and I love it.

During my pregnancy, they were always fussing over me, making sure I was comfortable, and I loved every minute of it. I'd get daily massages, and they always made sure the tub was hot for me. They kept me happy and fed.

They were extremely protective—more than usual. I had one guy with me all the damn time. I couldn't go anywhere without one of my mates being there constantly. They'd growl at anyone who got too close, supernatural or not. It'd freak the fuck out of the humans, and I almost felt bad for them, but you really can't trust anyone these days —human or supernatural.

"You ready, Katarina?" Ash asks as he walks into the bedroom. He's wearing a button-up and so is Nolan.

"Just waiting for Benji," I answer Ash. Benji comes out of the closet, finally dressed. It took him longer than me to find something to wear.

I get up from my vanity and look at my white dress adorned with red roses.

"We're all waiting outside." Az is behind Ash.

"Let's go see Ava graduate." I'm so excited to see her walk the stage. My daughter is all grown up.

"Tyler went to get Ezra, but I think they're held up by *playing just one more game.*" I knew Tyler shouldn't have been in charge of getting Ezra. Tyler likes his video games just like Ezra. They'll have late nights, and I have to tell Tyler not to do that on school nights.

"We're here," Tyler announces from the hallway. I grab Nolan from Ash and we make our way downstairs.

There's a van waiting for us. As we get in, Benji buckles Nolan in, and we're off to the school. It only takes us a few minutes since the school is on the property. There are shifters outside dressed just as nicely as we are.

When we get out, the principal greets us and walks us to our seats. Apparently we get the best seats. I don't mind it one bit. I want to be front and center to see Ava.

Ava's graduation is beautiful. They really go all out here, or maybe the guys are excited because they've come to love Ava like their own. They assure me Ezra will have something similar next year.

We've had a pre party and then the actual graduation party and apparently we're having another one tomorrow. The whole pack steps in and celebrates. I love the supportive community that my mates have built here.

I find Ryder, Bryson, Zayden, and Cash's family, and although they are part of the celebration, it still weighs on them heavily, as it does for us too. I wish they were able to see their kids graduate too.

After Ava walks the stage and the ceremony has ended, she comes to find us. Benji lifts her up and twirls her around before he gently puts her down. She laughs and smiles as we congratulate her, but the pain is still there; she just knows how to hide it better and blend in with the crowd.

I haven't seen Silas in a long time, and lately, I've kept replaying the conversation with Silas over and over in my head. It's starting to make sense now as I look into Ava's eyes.

"Are you ready for college?" Tyler asks her. She's going to be going to the same college Tyler attended, Mystic Shadow Academy. From what the guys tell me, there was a time when only the elite of the supernatural communities attended college. Times have changed, and though they let other students in, the elite families still have priority in enrollment.

Normally Ava's family would give her an easy in, but because she's lycan, we really had to convince the Dean that she wouldn't do anything to harm the other students and staff. We never told Ava about the strings we had to pull, and we never will. I don't want her to feel like an outcast.

It's hard to believe she's eighteen now and going off to college. "Mom, we did it." She hugs me tightly.

"This was all you," I remind her. She's been through more than any kid should go through, but she still managed to keep her grades up. I think school has been a welcomed distraction for her.

We may not know what happened to the guys, but for their sake, I hope they found peace.

Thank you so much for reading

If you enjoyed this book, please consider leaving a review.

Thank you!!!

Wait! Wait!! Wait!!!

Don't Panic!!!

Ava's story is definitely coming, but first, we've got the Wicked Succubus series to dive into. Stay tuned—Ava's epic adventure is on the horizon, and it's going to be super awesome!

Acknowledgments

Thank you to my Alpha and Beta Team for reading Chosen Wolf and giving me all the suggestions and feedback. I appreciate you ladies so much.

Thank you Heather for being on this journey with me and always helping get the cleanest possible manuscript to readers.

Thank you Ari. For always helping me. You're the best PA ever!!!

Thank you to my husband and my kids for giving me the time to write. I love you guys!

Thank you to my readers for reading Chosen Wolf. I had many ups and downs with this book and it took longer than anticipated but I wanted to bring you the best possible book to finish off the series.

I appreciate each and every one of you! I hope you enjoyed Kat and her men as much as I did! It was so much fun to write her character since she's so close to my age and thank you guys for showing this book and the characters all the love.

ALSO BY ANGELICA AQUILES

IRON BEAST PACK SERIES

Marked Wolf

https://amzn.to/3jYhRH5

Cursed Wolf

https://amzn.to/3v0WET3

Alphas' Origins

https://amzn.to/3JYpQ2R

Chosen Wolf

https://amzn.to/3CqHyc3

FAIRYTALES WITH A TWIST SERIES

The Dark Sea (Little Mermaid Retelling)

My Book

RISE OF THE DREADS SERIES

The Keepers Vengeance

My Book

Reign of Monsters

Wicked Succubus

My Book

About the Author

Angelica Aquiles currently lives in California, with her two sons, her husband, and her dog. She goes out fishing, hiking, and now off-roading with her family. When she has downtime she loves to get lost in a good book.

FB Group

https://www.facebook.com/groups/1107819209697422

Instagram

https://www.instagram.com/angelicaaquilesauthor/

TikTok

https://vm.tiktok.com/ZMdNa6nBy/

Bookbub

https://www.bookbub.com/authors/angelica-aquiles

Amazon Author Page

https://www.amazon.com/~/e/B091QFG3Y2

Goodreads

https://www.goodreads.com/angelicaaquilesauthor

Author Page
https://www.facebook.com/angelicaaquilesauthor/?notif_id=1623609310657351¬if_t=page_-fan&ref=notif